THE
NIGHT FLYERS

by
Elizabeth McDavid Jones

American Girl™

SCHOLASTIC INC.

New York Toronto London Auckland Sydney
Mexico City New Delhi Hong Kong Buenos Aires

HISTORY MYSTERIES

PICTURE CREDITS

The following organizations have generously given permission to reprint illustrations contained in "A Peek into the Past": p. 141 — U.S. Army Military History Institute, #3105-D8 36225; pp. 142-143 — State Historical Society of Wisconsin, #WHi W6 7409 (children); National Archives & Records Admin. (NARA), #165-WW-288C-14 (train); pp. 144-145 — NARA, #NWDNS-111-SC-107 (trench warfare) and #NWDNS-4-G-36(1) (soldier with pigeon); Armed Forces Collection, National Museum of American History, Smithsonian Institution (Cher Ami), U.S. Army Military History Institute, #3112-D8 36232 (lofts); pp. 146-147 — NARA, #NWDNS-4-P-200 (poster); Minnesota Historical Society, #435.12 r13 (rally); NARA, #NWDNS-165-WW-595D(14) (train) and #NWDNS-165-WW-595C(1) (stock boards); State Historical Society of Wisconsin, #WHi A62 6533 (city).

ISBN 0-439-38946-1

12 11 10 9 8 7 6 5 4 3 2 1   2 3 4 5 6 7/0

Printed in the U.S.A.   23

First Scholastic printing, January 2002

Cover: Paul Bachem
Map Illustration: Nenad Jakesevic
Line Art: Greg Dearth
Editor: Peg Ross
Art Direction: Laura Moberly and Jane Varda
Design: Laura Moberly and Pat Tuchscherer

To my husband, Rick,
and my children, Mandy, Lindsay,
Whitney, and Michael

TABLE OF CONTENTS

Little
Dismal
Swamp

Sanders'
cabin

Scuppernong Creek

Suggs farm

Lowder farm

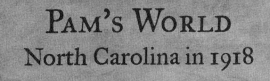

PAM'S WORLD
North Carolina in 1918

Currituck Sound

Currituck River

Currituck

CHAPTER I

A STRANGER

Do the rivers in France smell like the Currituck?

Pam Lowder drew a deep breath and lifted her eyes from her speller to the blue-gray waters of Currituck Sound. A breeze had wandered in the open window, carrying the sweet scent of bayberries from across the marsh.

I love the Currituck in fall, Pam thought. *The air's even more full of smells than in spring.*

The breeze barely stirred the closeness of the classroom, and she couldn't suppress a yawn. Miss Merrell's spelling lesson droned in Pam's ear until it mingled with the buzz of dirt daubers nesting on the windowsill outside.

Pam hated spelling. Why couldn't they study something interesting, like geography? She wanted to learn the names of the rivers in France, so she could write Papa and ask him if they *did* smell like the Currituck.

Pam pulled her eyes back inside, to the rows of desks

that kept the children of Currituck captive for five months
of the year. If Mama weren't so bent on Pam finishing
school, she could be out on the sound right now in her
skiff, fishing for white perch, or better yet, in her pigeon
loft at home, tending to the squeakers that had hatched
day before yesterday.

Miss Merrell was calling on the students in the sixth
speller to recite. "Alice," said Miss Merrell in her crispest
spelling-word tone. "Spell *mediocre*."

Alice Bagley stood up and recited without a moment's
hesitation.

"Thank you, Alice. That's correct."

"Show-off," Pam whispered under her breath, though
she knew she was being unfair. It wasn't Alice's fault if she
always had the right answers in class. It was just that Alice
was so sure of herself. But why shouldn't she be? She was
one of the smartest girls in the school and the most popu-
lar. Her father, as the postmaster, was the most influential
person in Currituck, aside from the sheriff. He also owned
the only drugstore in town and had been nice enough to
give Mama a job when Papa was drafted last year.

Miss Merrell had started calling on the fifth spellers,
those one book ahead of Pam. Sam Lewis. Fannie Rodgers.
Louisa White.

Pam knew it would soon be her turn. She tried to
study the words in her speller, but her thoughts kept
slipping out the window, to the robin's egg sky and the

shining Currituck Sound, and to Papa's last letter from . . . from "somewhere in France." That's all Papa was allowed to tell her and Mama about the location of his regiment in Europe. Papa was a doughboy in the American Expeditionary Force, which meant he was an American soldier helping the Allies in the war that seemed to have caught up the whole world.

Papa had been gone for many months, but he had only shipped overseas a few months ago. The rest of the time he had been training at Fort Monmouth in New Jersey, one of those tiny states up north. Last winter his letters from camp almost shivered with cold. Having lived in North Carolina all his life, he couldn't get used to the bitter cold of New Jersey.

So far he had written only once from France. Pam pulled Papa's letter from her dress pocket and reread (for the hundredth time) her favorite part:

> *The countryside is beautiful here, rich green meadows rolling up to cliffs that drop into the sea. The villages scattered along the coast look just like Currituck. Some of the villagers even keep homing pigeons, though nary a one is as handsome and strong as the Lowder pigeons.*

Pam could see Papa winking at her as he wrote that. It was a secret joke between them that other pigeon keepers could brag louder, but none could raise better pigeons

than she and Papa did. Maybe it was because they did it
for pure enjoyment, not to race them as most of the locals
did and, heaven forbid, not to fill somebody's dinner table.

"Pam Lowder."

Pam's mind lurched away from her pigeons back to the
classroom. Forty faces were staring at her, including Miss
Merrell's angry one. "You won't find the word spelled for
you in the sky outside the window."

Pam knew her expression was as blank as the tablet in
front of her. Which word had Miss Merrell called for her
to spell? The boys across the aisle from her were starting
to snicker.

"We're waiting," said Miss Merrell.

Pam made herself stand. Her mind raced. Which word?
Which word?

"*Locust.*" A whisper from somewhere behind her. "Spell
locust."

Was it Nina? Best friends were for moments like these,
weren't they? Pam started to spell, hesitantly at first.

"L-O-C . . ." She stopped to think. Was it *o* next? Or *u*?

Titters drifted across the aisle. Pam shot the boys a
dirty look and continued. "U-S . . ."

She paused again. There were snickers behind her now.
Miss Merrell was glaring at her. *They think I can't finish the
word*, Pam thought.

"T," she said loudly, to convince everyone she had been
sure of the word all along.

The classroom burst into laughter. Pam felt her face flame.

"I suppose this is your idea of a joke, Pam." Miss Merrell's voice had taken on the icy tone she reserved for spitball throwers and other transgressors of schoolhouse law. "I would never have expected such behavior from you."

"Ma'am?" Pam was perplexed. "What behavior?"

"Don't act innocent with me, young lady. I called out *encyclopedia*. You spelled *locust*. Purposefully answering my questions incorrectly may get laughs from your classmates, but it also gets you thirty minutes in the corner after school. Standing on one leg. Now, let's try to get on with our lesson." With a hand on each hip, she turned to the other side of the room. "Linwood, spell *encyclopedia*."

Pam knew the matter was closed. She sank into her seat and tried to hide behind Nancy Carlton's head. Which wasn't easy, considering Pam was the tallest—and oldest—student in fourth grade.

A black funk settled over her like a swarm of flies. How many times had Mama warned her about daydreaming in class?

"You can't afford to miss any more lessons than what you do when you stay out to help me on the farm," Mama had said only last week. "Make Papa proud of all you've learned when he gets home from the war."

Make Papa proud of you. The words rang through her head. And look what she'd gone and done. Made a fool of herself in front of the whole school and gotten herself in trouble to boot. Papa surely wouldn't be proud of her now.

Who had played such a dirty trick on her?

Pam stole a glance behind her. Her eyes met Nina's, and Nina jerked her head to the left and back one more row, toward Henry Bagley, Alice's bratty younger brother. Henry, legs in the aisle, hands behind his neck, was grinning like a possum. When he saw Pam looking at him, he mouthed "*locust*" and doubled over with silent laughter.

Henry! Who else?

He made it a point to get Pam's goat every chance he got. And he didn't even have to work at it. Henry just being Henry was enough. The worst thing was, Pam had to put up with him because Mama worked for his father. Mama agreed that Henry was a pain, but she called him "an affliction" Pam would have to bear.

Pam tilted her head and smiled sweetly back at Henry, but she filled her eyes with venom.

He stuck out his tongue.

When Miss Merrell finally released Pam, the school yard had cleared out. Pam was glad she didn't have to see the other kids. Then she spotted loyal Nina sitting under the chinaberry tree, eating a biscuit from her tin lunch-pail. Nina hopped to her feet as Pam dragged down the schoolhouse steps.

"You were in there a long time."

"Yeah." Pam knew Nina wanted details. After all, they usually told each other everything. But Pam couldn't this time. She just couldn't.

"Want some of my collard biscuit?" Nina asked, as the girls climbed over the stile in the school yard fence.

"No, thanks. I'm not hungry."

"Well, what did she say to you?"

"I don't want to talk about it," said Pam.

"Why? Did you get a whipping?"

"No!" said Pam adamantly. A sigh escaped from the depths of her soul. "She stood me in the corner and lectured me on behaving in a fit manner for a soldier's daughter. It made me feel awful. She said I was letting Papa down by not applying myself and by being a smart aleck."

"Didn't you tell her what Henry did?"

"No use. I'd still be in trouble for not paying attention. I might as well admit it, when it comes to school, I'm a dolt."

"No, you're not."

Pam forced a smile. "Thanks, Nina, but it's true. I'm two grades behind Alice Bagley. And she's twelve, same as me."

"It's not your fault. You have to stay out of school so much to help your parents on the farm. You come to school a lot more than the other farm kids. Look at your neighbors, Buell and Mattie Suggs. They can't even read."

"That's different. They're tenant farmers. Their ma and pa think school's a waste of time because those kids can't hope for anything more than farming someone else's land. Mattie acts like she don't care, but I know she wishes she could read."

The girls had reached Nina's front gate. She lived next to the courthouse, a block down Main Street from the school. Nina's father, Judge Patterson, was the only lawyer in Currituck County. Since cases in sleepy little Currituck were few, he worked mostly in Elizabeth City, forty miles across the Albemarle Sound.

"You want to come in for a while?" Nina asked.

Pam shook her head. "Can't. I'm already late meeting Mama at the store. Maybe tomorrow."

Pam continued down Main Street, the only real street in town, unless you counted the rutted lane that ran by the lumber mill and the steamer dock and stopped dead at the river. The few businesses in town—the general store and the dry goods, the drugstore, the bank, Purdy's Grain and Seed—were scattered along Main. The entire street was barely half a mile long, but the drugstore was way at the other end.

Pam picked up her pace, hoping to reach the drugstore before she saw anyone she would have to talk to. She passed Doc Weston's house with his tiny office in back, then the Farm Bureau. At the general store, Pam noticed two new posters in the window. One poster announced the community patriotic meeting for the week, a public "singing" on Saturday night in the opera house above the store.

The second poster, Pam knew, was just meant to stir up people to buy government bonds to pay for the war. Still, it made her shudder. A devilish German soldier clutched a dagger dripping with blood. "Beat Back the Hun with Liberty Bonds," the poster proclaimed. An image flashed into her head: Papa in battle, crawling on his belly through no-man's-land, while the Hun with his dagger waited over the next rise. She pushed the image from her mind. *I won't think about that,* she told herself. *Papa knows how to defend himself against the Germans. Mama said so.*

She couldn't help worrying about him, though. If only the Allies would hurry up and win the war so Papa could come home. She had read in the newspaper only last week that the Germans were retreating in France. Folks were saying it was the beginning of the end, though Mama told Pam not to get her hopes up. Wars took a lot longer to finish than they did to get started, she said.

Pam sighed. If only Papa could come home, everything would be back to normal again. But the Hun on the poster gloated at her. *Your papa won't come home if I have anything to do with it,* it seemed to say. Anger and resentment surged through her. The Germans were barbarians! They must be—dragging the world into war and taking girls' fathers away from them!

Pam felt gloomier than ever. She was in no mood to
see Alice and her friends Louisa White and Fannie
Rodgers strolling down the sidewalk toward her. Pam
could hear their laughter even from where she stood. Alice
had gotten her hair bobbed in Norfolk last week, and she
was wearing a new white dress from the Sears-Roebuck
catalogue. Pam's cotton dress and scuffed brogans, which
usually suited her fine, made her feel more awkward than
ever next to stylish Alice.

Alice and her friends walked abreast, and there was no
way Pam could avoid them. Rudeness was a sin in Currituck;
if Alice spoke to her, she would have to speak back. Alice
was friendly to Pam at the drugstore, but at school she
seldom ventured out of her circle of friends. Maybe she
would be too absorbed in conversation to notice Pam.

No such luck. "Hey, Pam," said Alice. Louisa and
Fannie echoed Alice's greeting but continued to whisper
and giggle.

Pam was sure they were talking about her, laughing
at her for making a fool of herself at school. "Hey," she
muttered. She lifted a hand in greeting but strode past
without saying anything more.

She found Mama sorting mail in the post office, which
was just a back room of the drugstore. "Anything from
Papa?" Pam asked.

Mama shook her head. "Nothing." Her lips were set
in a line.

"Shouldn't we have heard *something* from him? Just a line or two to let us know how he is?" Pam's stomach churned. Was Mama worried about Papa too?

"I'm sure we'll hear directly, sugar. Papa don't have much chance to get mail out to us, is all." She touched Pam's cheek and brushed aside a wisp of hair that had escaped from Pam's braids. "Why the long face?"

Pam told Mama what had happened at school. "I'm not going back," she insisted. "I'll be more use to you at home than I am in that schoolhouse. I'd have the house cleaned and supper cooked before you got home at night. Then you could sit in your rocker and rest up from working all day."

"I'll not have my daughter keeping my house while I loll around with my feet propped up."

"Mattie does all the housekeeping at her house," said Pam.

"So she does, poor li'l thing." Mama clucked. "Fond as I am of Iva Suggs, I think she's done wrong by those younguns keeping 'em out of school. Just 'cause she and Ralph never had a day's schooling in their lives is no reason to deny an education to their younguns.

"Times ain't like they was when Iva and me was growing up. This war is changing everything, even in Currituck. Young folks need an education to get on in life now. Papa and I have hopes for you, Pam, to go on to high school and make something of yourself."

"High school?" This was a new notion to Pam, and she wasn't sure she liked it. She'd never thought much beyond the boundaries of the one-room schoolhouse and Currituck County. "Then I'd have to board in Norfolk or Elizabeth City. I'd have to leave you and Papa and Currituck."

"I'm not saying you have to. We only want you to have a choice. And the way to have a choice is to stay in school and do your best."

"I do try, Mama. I try to stuff my head full of all that book learning, but it seems to slip away as fast as I stuff it in. I have to work twice as hard as the other kids just to keep up."

"Nothing worthwhile ever comes easy," said Mama.

"*Nothing* comes easy to me."

"That's not true. Animals come easy to you. Why, it's almost like magic the way you can tame a coon as if it was a kitten, and have wild jays flying down and sitting on your shoulder. And look what you done with your pigeons. Who else has a loft of pigeons that will home at night in the worst of weather? You've got a gift, Pam. You do."

"What use is a gift like that?"

"Hold on till I finish this mail, sugar, and I'll tell you how much your gift is worth." She stuck the last few letters in boxes and sat down beside Pam. "A man showed up in town today, a stranger. He was dressed peculiar—clear he wasn't from around here. He drove his motor truck up and down the street, like he was looking for something, and then he finally stopped in front of the general store and went in. Miz Gracie Langley happened to be in here getting some headache powders, and she nearly had a fit to know what his business was. She hustled to the general store straightaway and come back so flustered she could hardly talk. She kept sputtering about his accent. Flat out begged Mr. Bagley to send a telegram to the CPI right away to report the man."

Pam was alarmed. "The CPI—isn't that the government agency that hunts down . . ." Her voice trailed into the air. It was too scary to think about the answer to her question.

"Yes. Spies," Mama finished for her. "Miz Gracie is convinced the man's a German spy."

CHAPTER 2
SPIES IN CURRITUCK?

Pam drew in a sharp breath. A German spy! Here in Currituck! There had been rumors of German U-boats lurking off the North Carolina coast, but since no one had actually seen one Mama said it was only idle talk, people's fears being put into words.

Pam's heart hammered in her chest. "Mama, do you think . . . ?"

"No, I don't," said Mama. "An accent don't make a person a German, and it sure don't make 'em a spy. Mr. Bagley politely told Miz Gracie her notion was hogwash."

"He did?" Pam couldn't imagine gracious Mr. Bagley saying anything of the sort.

Mama smiled. "Not in those words, of course. Naturally Miz Gracie wouldn't listen to reason. Claimed she was still going to report the man, and she warned us not to tell him too much in the meantime, though I don't know what in heaven's name she thinks *we* could tell him. Look out for the weevils on the cotton crop? We're farmers and fishermen here, not soldiers."

Pam's dread vanished with Mama's joke. She laughed. "But what does the stranger have to do with me?"

"I'm getting to that. The man found his way to the drugstore 'long about midmorning. And it was queer, very queer, because I don't know how he knew."

"Knew what?"

"About your pigeons."

"My pigeons?"

Mama nodded. "He wanted to buy your pigeons. All of 'em. The whole loft."

Pam was horrified. "You didn't sell my birds, did you?"

"They're not mine to sell. Papa gave the loft to you when he was called up to service. I told the man he'd have to talk to you."

Pam thought about that. A mysterious stranger come to town, a man who had the whole town buzzing, and he wanted to buy *her* pigeons. It did make her feel important.

"Come on, honey," Mama said. "Mr. Bagley's waiting on us to close up." She beckoned for Pam to follow her into the drugstore. "Oh, by the way, Iva Suggs is down with another spell. Buell come in this morning looking for Doc Weston. The stranger ended up toting Buell off in his motor truck to find the doctor. 'Course, when Miz Gracie found out, she said it'd be the last we'd see of Buell." Mama shook her head. "Such foolishness."

Mr. Bagley was washing glasses at the soda fountain and stacking them on the counter. "I sent Henry out to your place earlier to cut you some stove wood," he said, beaming. "Should be a stack waiting on your porch."

Pam cringed. Why did Mr. Bagley insist on having Henry do their chores? Pam knew he was trying to be nice, but his constant charity embarrassed her, and she hated feeling beholden to Henry.

If Mama felt the same way, she never hinted at it. "We're obliged," she told him. "That'll give us leave to get right down to cooking supper. Won't it, Pam?"

"Yes, ma'am," Pam said, hurrying out the door before Mama or Mr. Bagley could see the insincerity in her face. She'd rather eat straw than burn wood chopped by Henry Bagley, and that was the truth. Why did she have to pretend she felt one way when she really felt the opposite? Grown-ups expected you to be honest, except when being honest was rude. Then it was all right to be dishonest—but only a little. She shook her head. She would never understand grown-ups.

Mama was lingering inside, talking to Mr. Bagley. Pam couldn't help overhearing. Mr. Bagley fairly boomed. He was saying something about a Red Cross meeting tomorrow, about packing Currituck preserves to send to the starving Belgians. "Imagine the Germans starving little children," Pam heard him say. "It's inhuman, just inhuman."

"Pa's talking Germans again, ain't he?" It was Alice,

though Pam hadn't noticed her approach. "I think he
wishes *he* was a soldier." She chuckled at her father.

Pam didn't laugh. "You should be glad he's not over
there."

Alice's smile vanished. "I'm sorry, Pam. I forgot about
your pa for a minute. Listen, I tried to tell you earlier"—
she emphasized the word *earlier*—"that I didn't think
Henry's little joke this afternoon was funny at all. I hope
you noticed I wasn't laughing."

"No, I didn't really notice," said Pam. She wished Alice
hadn't brought it up again. She wanted to forget the whole
thing.

"Well, if you need help in spelling, just ask me. I'll be
glad to tutor you anytime."

Alice's offer, meant kindly, sliced deep into Pam's
pride. *So Alice thinks I'm a dolt too.* It wasn't worth trying to
explain that she would've known how to spell the word if
she'd known which word the teacher called out. "Thanks,"
Pam choked out, "but I doubt Mama can spare me from
the farm right now."

The awkward moment was cut short—thankfully—
when Mama finally came out of the store. Pam couldn't
have been more glad to say good-bye to Alice and leave
with Mama.

They walked the mile to Scuppernong Creek where
their small, flat-bottomed boat, called a skiff, was moored.
The Scuppernong was one of the many small creeks that

fed the Currituck River, which in turn flowed into Currituck Sound. The Scuppernong was named for the vines that twined among the trees on the creek's edge and bore luscious fat grapes in early fall. A few miles upcreek they passed Buell Suggs and his little brothers Marvin and Rupert seining for bass. Buell and Marvin hauled the net, or seine, into their boat while Rupert rowed forward just enough to keep the net from tangling. Their catch was poor, fewer than seventy pounds, Pam guessed.

"How's your ma doing, Buell?" Mama asked.

Buell pulled the net inside out, releasing the thrashing fish into the bottom of the boat. Though he was only fourteen, his back and arms were knotted with muscles from working hard ever since he was old enough to walk behind a plow. Now that his mother was sick and his father away at war, Buell had to man the farm and feed the family with only his brothers' help.

"She's tolerable," Buell said. "Doc says she'll be down at least a couple weeks. Nursing the twins has pure sapped her strength. She needs to drink lots of milk, he says."

Pam and Mama exchanged glances. They both knew the puny Suggs cow gave barely enough milk for all the Suggs youngsters. There would be none left over for Iva. Pam noticed Buell's fingers twitching nervously on the net. He was asking for their help. Pam thought it must be an awful burden to have that much responsibility at Buell's age.

"You're welcome to half what Daisy gives every day," Mama offered. Daisy was one of their cows. The other, Lula, was ready to drop a calf any day.

Tension drained from Buell's face. "I thank ya, Miz Lowder. Ma figured that. She done sent Mattie over to your place to borrow some milk. Mattie's probably waiting on you now."

Dusk was falling fast when Pam and Mama reached home. Without speaking, they trudged from the creek up the wooded slope to the backyard. As they neared the house, they could hear the porch swing creaking around front and Mattie singing the refrain of "Amazing Grace." Pam climbed the back stairs and splashed water from the washbasin on her sweaty face. Soon Mattie appeared. "Henry Bagley was here," she said by way of greeting. "Cut y'all a stack of wood, but he hightailed it right off. That boy ain't friendly, is he?"

"Why? What did he say?" Pam asked. She dried her hands and face with the salt sack hung on a nail above the washbasin.

"That's just it. Wouldn't say nothing. Acted like he was too good to talk to me." Mattie dearly loved to talk. She would have taken that as a high insult. She could talk for hours solid if she had a listener. But how could you fault her? She went all day long with nothing but noses to wipe and chores to do, and Iva Suggs wasn't one to waste time in idle chatter.

"Consider yourself lucky," said Pam. "I'm glad he's gone. He's the *last* person I want to talk to."

"You don't like him?"

"It's a long story," said Pam. "I'll tell you while we're milking Daisy. I need to change clothes first."

Mattie followed Pam into her bedroom. Pam dumped her book sack on her bed. While she changed into her overalls and hung up her school dress, Mattie studied the giant map of Europe Pam had tacked to her wall. The map was dotted in red to show the movement of American troops across England and France. Big blue stars showed places in France where Pam thought Papa might have been: Château-Thierry on the Marne River, Soissons, Cantigny on the Somme River, Belleau Wood. Mattie touched the stars gingerly with her fingertips. Her father was in the same regiment as Papa. Mattie probably figured he had been in those places too.

"No new stars since the last time I was here," Mattie said sadly.

Pam was lacing up an old pair of Papa's boots that she wore to do her chores. The toes were stuffed with newspaper to keep the boots from flopping. "Nope. Ain't had no more letters." She tried to sound unconcerned, but it was hard to keep her voice from cracking.

"Oh." Mattie's voice hung heavy with disappointment. "I was hoping you'd have a new one to read me." Since Mattie's father couldn't read or write, the family rarely heard from him. "I like to pretend your letters are mine, from Pa. It's easy if I take out your name and put mine in. Except for the pigeon parts." She made a face, which Pam ignored. Mattie didn't like pigeons, even though Buell had a loft of his own.

"I'll get the map up-to-date next week after we get a copy of Sunday's *Gazette*. You can help if you want," Pam offered.

Mattie accepted eagerly. She chattered behind Pam through the kitchen and out to the barn, and continued to chatter while Pam settled against Daisy's side and began milking. Pam was used to Mattie's constant talking. After all, they'd known each other all their lives. Most of the time it didn't bother her, but tonight she could barely tolerate it. For once, Pam wanted to do the talking. The incident with Henry at school lay in her chest like a millstone. Maybe Mattie would understand how awkward she felt at school, like a gangly colt trying to walk. She broke in to Mattie's chatter and told her what had happened.

Instead of sympathizing, Mattie started to scold. "What do you expect, Pam? I don't see why you even bother with school. You ain't never going to catch up with them town kids. They got nothing to do but stick their noses in books all the time, not like you and me. What you going to do with all that book learning anyway? It's a waste of time for a girl. Like you always messin' with critters. That stuff's for boys."

Angry words flew to Pam's lips, but she bit them back. Mattie was only echoing what she heard at home. Instead, Pam changed the subject. "Come up and see my new squeakers, Mattie. The one's just a little ball of fluff, but he tries to act so fierce." She tried to swallow the hurt sticking in her throat from Mattie's retort.

"You still got that wild dog hanging 'round your bird shed?" Mattie was scared of Bosporus, the wild dog Pam had been taming.

"He won't mess with you," said Pam. "He's getting tamer every day."

"That's all right. I'll go on up to the house and see your ma. I best be getting home soon anyway."

Pam poured half of Daisy's milk into another pail and gave it to Mattie. Then she headed to the pigeon loft to care for her pigeons. The barn and most of the outbuildings—the toolshed, the smokehouse, the corncrib, the privy—sat at the bottom of the slope near the woods, but Papa had built the pigeon loft near the house, by a thicket of myrtle bushes. A true pigeoneer, Papa said, wants to be close to his birds. Pam felt the same way. With her pigeons she felt none of the awkwardness she suffered at school. She felt confident and in control. Caring for them had become second nature to her. Papa had raised her around the birds; he called her his "right-hand Pam."

Animals were so much easier than school, Pam thought. With animals, there was no need to wonder if you were right or wrong. They let you know right off if you had done the right thing by the way they responded. And you could feel your way to correct a mistake, not like in school where you might struggle on and on with an arithmetic problem and find out in the end you had done it all wrong. With animals, gentleness and confidence always worked; there was no guesswork involved. That was her gift with animals, she thought. That's all it was.

Then Pam heard the *ierh ierh* of distressed pigeons, and her senses were instantly alert. She rushed to the loft. Some of the young pigeons were flapping about outside in the screened fly-pen, crying loudly. Inside the loft, the older birds were a little more noisy than usual, but not visibly upset. A few flapped about in the bath pan on the floor, and some were perched in the roosting boxes that lined the rear wall, preening their feathers. Her best birds, the flock leaders, were sitting calmly in their nesting boxes, tending their squeakers. Her favorite cock, copper-colored Caspian, blinked knowingly at her as he sat brooding on the nest pan. Male and female pigeons shared equally in family responsibilities; Caspian was giving his mate Odessa a chance to bathe.

Caspian was Pam's most even-tempered bird. He tapped her lightly with his beak and cooed, as if to reassure her that he had everything under control. Papa had called Caspian Billy Boy, but when the war broke out four years ago, he let Pam rename the birds for European landmarks. She liked the strange but beautiful sounds of the names, and they seemed to fit all her animals.

She was a little puzzled at the behavior of the pigeons in the fly-pen, but she shrugged it off. Young pigeons were easily spooked; any unusual noise could have set them off.

Then something crashed outside. The loft erupted in pigeon scolding. Pam's eyes snapped to the window, and she grinned. Bosporus, still a clumsy youngster, had knocked over feeding troughs stacked in the lean-to that adjoined the loft on the opposite side from the fly-pen. Pam had been training him to watch over her birds, and he took the job seriously. He looked out for the pigeons as if they were his own pups.

Pam talked gently to the birds to quiet them. One of the squeakers, who had not yet learned to fly, hopped on her shoulder as she cleaned his nest compartment.

"You need a name, little feller," she said. "I'll call you Belleau, after that battle I read about in the newspaper a while back." She didn't know for sure, but Pam thought Papa had probably fought in the Battle of Belleau Wood. It was the first major battle Pam knew about where American troops had driven back the Germans.

Thoughts of Papa set her heart to aching. What fun she and Papa had taking care of the birds together! He would have been so pleased to know their pigeons had drawn the attention of the stranger in town.

"I'll write Papa tonight and tell him," she told Belleau. Belleau squeaked his approval.

Pam flipped the trapdoor in the ceiling of the loft. The birds poured through the opening and whirred into the air. Homing pigeons needed plenty of exercise to stay strong and sleek; all pigeoneers knew that. But Papa had learned that more exercise also made his birds better breeders, so Lowder pigeons were in great demand among local keepers as breeding stock.

Little Belleau maintained his perch on Pam's shoulder as she went to the lean-to to get barley and peas for the pigeons' feeding trough. Bosporus trotted over and nudged Pam for attention.

"Always into something, ain't ya, boy?" she asked affectionately. She scratched the sensitive spot under his muzzle.

Suddenly he cocked his head and barked sharply. Little Belleau squeaked pitifully and flapped his wings.

"Bos!" Pam scolded. "How many times do I have to tell you not to bark around the birds!"

Then a voice rang from the darkness. "I would think such conduct was natural." A man stepped into the ring of light cast by Pam's lantern. "For a dog."

He spoke with a foreign accent.

CHAPTER 3
A SURPRISING OFFER

The image of the Hun on the poster flashed into Pam's head, and fear clutched at her throat. "Who are you?" she choked out.

"Arminger," said the man, casually, as if he wasn't the least bit interested in his own name. He was staring at Bosporus. "Beautiful animal, though I don't recognize the breed. What is he?" He reached a hand toward the dog. Bosporus growled.

Pam's answer was guarded. "Part setter. Part wolf." She emphasized the word *wolf.* "Why are you here?" She was careful to keep Bos between them.

"Yah, I can see the setter in him, and the wolf, now that you mention it. The strong haunches, the thick shoulders . . . yah." Arminger nodded and took the cigarette he was smoking from his mouth. "Gorgeous animal." He paused a moment, then went on. "But I came to see your birds. Your mother gave consent. I'm new in Currituck, you see, and I'm thinking of raising some pigeons."

So Mama had given him leave to come see her, which meant she wasn't worried about Arminger. *Maybe I'm fretting over nothing,* thought Pam. She glanced at Mama's figure passing in front of the lighted kitchen window. What should she do if the man did offer to buy her birds? Did Mama want her to sell them? They needed the money badly. *Cross that bridge when you come to it,* she thought.

The least she could do was show this Arminger around. Besides, it would give her a chance to "talk pigeons," which she hadn't been able to do since Papa left. Pam willed herself to relax. "Come on in the loft. You'll see it's big for the number of birds I got. Maybe it looks like an ordinary shed on the outside, but inside I think it's real special." She held the loft door open and waved Arminger in. "My papa says giving pigeons breathing space makes 'em healthier. So does fresh air and sunlight. That's why he put in windows on one wall and attached the fly-pen to one side of the loft. An opening between lets the birds go in and out of the fly-pen whenever they want. Except when the weather's bad. Then I close the opening off."

Arminger started into the loft eagerly, but nearly tripped when Bosporus squeezed ahead of him. "You let your dog in with your pigeons?"

"I'm training him as my guard dog. I taught him not to act like a dog around the birds. Barking and pigeons don't mix."

"I'm impressed," said Arminger. "A dog learning not to be a dog."

The words of praise sent a tingle of warmth through Pam's body. Here was someone who appreciated her skill with animals. So he sounded a little peculiar, the way he talked in his throat and dropped his *r*'s. That didn't make him a German. Mama had said so. He was nothing like the Hun on the poster. And he knows animals, Pam told herself emphatically. He can't be too bad.

Her wariness began to evaporate, and "pigeon talk" simply slipped out of her mouth. "There's swamps all around here, and the weather's wet and windy, not the best climate for pigeons. See how the loft is open only on the side that has the fly-pen, and that side's sheltered by myrtle bushes? Protects the pigeons from drafts, and the sloping roof and overhang keeps even the fly-pen dry as a bone." She felt like Mattie, prattling on, but Arminger hung on every word. He would be a good pigeoneer, thought Pam. He noticed things most people wouldn't, like the condition of a bird's feathers, the keenness of its eye, or just the fact that every bird was different—in coloring, in build, in personality.

By the time Pam had finished showing Arminger around the loft, the moon had risen. "It's late," she told him. "I best be calling my birds and getting in to supper."

"I've kept you too long. Will your mother be worried?"

"No," Pam said, without a second thought. She realized

that *she* wasn't worried either. Not at all. She had a feeling Arminger could be trusted.

"That's good," he said. His *th* sounded like a *d,* and his *d* sounded like a *t.* He took a long draw on his cigarette and blew the smoke into a cloud that was swallowed by the darkness. "Because there's one thing more I'm curious about. Granted, I don't know that much about pigeons. But I'm an observant fellow, and I particularly notice animals. I'm fond of animals—all kinds—and I think you are, too, Pam, yah?"

Pam nodded, but she was perplexed. What was he leading up to? There was more than his speech that was peculiar about this man.

For long moments he stood silent, puffing on his cigarette. Curiosity screamed inside her head for him to finish what he'd started to say, but courtesy demanded that she wait until he was ready.

Finally he continued. "One thing I've noticed about birds, Pam, and maybe you have too, is that they never fly at night. Except for owls, of course."

Understanding flooded Pam's brain. "Oh, you're wondering why my pigeons are night flyers," she said.

"Exactly."

The words rushed out of Pam's mouth. "Papa's really a herring fisherman. The farm's to feed us, y'see, and fishing brings in the cash money. Like with most folks around here, we do a little bit of everything to survive. Sometimes

Papa had to be out all night on the water, and he knew
Mama worried about him. So he trained the pigeons to
carry messages home to her through the dark to set her
mind at ease. When the birds trap back through the trapdoor into the loft, it rings that bell"—Pam nodded toward
a bell hanging under the eaves—"and Mama can hear it
from the kitchen."

"Uh-huh." Arminger's eyes were bright with interest.
"And how did your papa train them to fly in the dark?"

"He started out training 'em to trap into the loft like
you would ordinary homers. Then the morning flights was
made earlier and earlier and the evening flights later and
later till both was being done in the dark. Thing was, Papa
had to toss the birds hard into the air when he let 'em go
for their training flights. Else they'd have followed their
instinct to roost in the dark rather than fly."

"And you helped him with all of this?"

"Ever since I was little. Shoot, I could barely walk when
Papa had me out here cleaning nest boxes and measuring
grain. The older I got, the more he let me handle the birds
and help with their training, till I reckon I was doing near
as much as him. Then, when he went off to soldier last fall,
he gave me the loft to manage on my own." Pam's voice
cracked when she mentioned Papa's leaving. She coughed
quickly, hoping Arminger hadn't noticed. She didn't want
him to think she was a crybaby. Arminger treated her as
an equal, practically. No one else had ever done that. She

wanted to hold on to the feeling.

"And you've done well, very well indeed. I'm sure your papa will be proud of you when he returns from the war." Arminger paused. His jaw worked back and forth. "I've got an offer for you, Pam."

The roar of the cicadas suddenly rose, or was the roaring only in Pam's ears? She knew what Arminger's offer was going to be, and she wasn't sure she wanted to hear it.

"I want to buy your birds, Pam, all your trained birds. I'll give you two hundred dollars for the lot."

Two hundred dollars! A fortune! Pam's mind raced. With that much money, Mama could stop working. They could hire a man to help out with the heavy farmwork, which would mean no more being beholden to Henry Bagley. Two hundred dollars for her pigeons!

Pam gazed up at the sky, where the shadows of her pigeons winged across the moon. Pride welled inside her. All the hours she and Papa put in training and caring for those birds had paid off. They were the strongest and smartest homers in the county, and she knew it. Yet they were more like friends to her than animals. How could she sell bold Caspian and perky little Odessa, his mate? Or the proud Orleans and his silvery hen Verdun? How could she sell any of her best birds?

"I don't think so, Mr. Arminger," Pam told the man.

"Why not?" Arminger's voice had an irritated edge. "It's a solid offer. You won't get more money anywhere else."

"Oh, I know. It's not the money. I just don't want to sell 'em. That's all." Pam was a little irritated herself. How could he think money was the only thing she had to consider? *If he was really an animal lover,* Pam thought with disdain, *he'd understand how I feel about my birds.*

"Well, think about it," he said. "I'll contact you later." Then he was gone.

Pam stood staring into the darkness where Arminger had melted into the night. "*Contact* me?" she whispered. "Peculiar, that he is." She wondered if he would reappear just as mysteriously. "Oh, well," she said, shrugging her shoulders. But she couldn't shrug away the presence Arminger had left behind.

Pam rattled the pigeons' feeding can to call them back to the loft. They dropped from the sky onto the landing board on the roof and wasted no time trapping through the door. She fed and watered them and closed up the loft for the night.

The smell of sizzling bacon greeted her in the kitchen. Mama was bent over the big black range, pulling a skillet of cornbread from the oven. "Been keeping your supper warm," she said. "Sit down and eat."

"Mattie gone?" Pam asked. She took her place at the table as Mama put a steaming plate of bacon and potatoes in front of her. Pam's mouth watered furiously, and she realized she was starving. It must be very late.

"Buell came and fetched her," said Mama. "He wanted

to know if he could borrow some of Papa's crab pots tomorrow." She sat across from Pam and bit into a square of cornbread. She didn't say a word about Arminger's visit. Pam knew Mama was waiting until she was ready to talk. Mama had the patience of Job, Papa always said. Pam wished she could be more like her mother in that way.

"The man—his name is Arminger—offered to buy my birds," Pam said.

"I figured he would. How much?"

"Two hundred dollars."

"Lordy mercy." Mama put down her fork. "That's a heap of money for some pigeons."

Guilt was slowly creeping through Pam's body. Two hundred dollars would go a far piece toward making Mama's life easier. Maybe it was selfish to think only of her own love for the birds. "Should I sell 'em to him?"

"That's up to you, sugar. What'd you tell him?"

"I told him no. But he said for me to think about it. Said he'd contact me later."

"Mmm." Mama screwed up her face. She was thinking. "If you don't want to sell 'em, it's settled."

"But we could use the money, couldn't we?"

"There's always a use for money," said Mama. "We've made do so far, and we'll keep making do. Don't you fret your head about it. Besides, we don't really know nothin' about this . . . this Mr. Arminger."

Did Mama distrust Arminger? If she did, she would

never say so, for fear of scaring Pam. Pam's uneasiness returned. "You think he's a German, Mama?"

She was slow to answer. "I don't know; never known one. I do know the Germans here in America ain't the same as the ones fighting your papa, never mind all the talk you hear."

"You don't think he's a spy, though?"

"Can't imagine what a spy would spy on way out here in these woods. But wartime means hard times, Pam, and hard times mean no-account characters hanging about where they don't belong. Who knows where he got all that money he offered you, or if he even has it for sure. Could be he's a slacker dodging the draft or a deserter from one of the army camps. Could be we'll never see hide nor hair of him again. We don't know. You just steer clear of him from now on, you hear?"

CHAPTER 4
DISGRACED AGAIN

Lula's labor pains came on late in the night, and she woke Pam up with her bellowing. At first Pam and Mama thought they would lose both Lula and the calf, but she finally delivered a healthy baby that afternoon. Pam named the calf Pyrenees, after a mountain range in France. Now that both Lula and her baby were safe, Pam was glad the crisis had given her an excuse to miss school. She dreaded the thought of going back.

Since they were home in the middle of the day, Mama suggested they visit the Suggses and see what they could do for Iva. The day was overcast, so it was a cool walk through the browning fields to the Suggs place. The Suggs family grew tobacco for Mr. Eugene Swindell. Mr. Eugene lived in a mansion in Norfolk and showed his face in Currituck only twice a year to collect his rent.

The Suggses' house was built like most tenant

dwellings, in "shotgun" style, with a hallway running from front to back. You could shoot a shotgun through the front door straight out the back, folks joked. The house was dwarfed by a huge live oak that shaded its swept-clean yard. As usual, there was a horde of dirty children playing out front. "Go on in, Miz Lowder," a voice called from above their heads. Pam looked up; it was Rupert, perched on a limb high in the oak tree, bare feet dangling. "Ma's in the bed, but she ain't sleeping."

"Thank you, Rupert," said Mama. "Don't you fall now."

"No, ma'am. Ain't fell once yet."

"Where's Mattie?" Pam called up the tree.

"Oh, she can't come out," Rupert said. "Ma's got her shelling beans in the kitchen. 'Sides, she's minding the twins."

A baby wailed inside, and Pam heard someone hollering Mattie's name. Poor Mattie! Never a minute to herself. Pam considered going in to help. Then she thought of the cramped Suggs kitchen that always smelled of sour dishrags. She hesitated as her conscience pricked at her, but in the end she ignored its nagging and went down to have a look at Buell's pigeons. Buell had started his loft and his rabbit hutches with the idea of making extra money by breeding the animals and selling them. That was about the time his father got drafted, Pam remembered. She didn't figure he'd had time to do much with them since.

Buell kept his birds in an old toolshed he had fitted

with nesting compartments. The floor of the shed hadn't been cleaned in a while, and his puny birds—there were only eight—moved about sluggishly. Their grit pan was empty, and their drinking water was cloudy. One blue checkered hen sat lifelessly with her feathers fluffed. She's dead, Pam thought; then the hen blinked its dull, black eyes. Pitiful little thing!

Rage rose in Pam's chest. How could Buell treat his pigeons this way?

True, Buell had to pull the weight of a full-grown man, but Pam couldn't excuse him neglecting his animals. At least he could keep the shed clean.

She marched out to find Buell, talking to herself. "He don't feed 'em proper, he don't exercise 'em, he don't hardly spend no time with 'em. Why does he even bother to keep 'em?" She spied Buell hiding in back of his rabbit hutches, smoking. Figured. Buell was more interested in playacting like he was grown than in taking care of his animals. Pam tried to hold her voice steady as her heart thumped in her throat. "Your mama know you're smoking?"

"Reckon I can do what I want. I'm the man around here," Buell snarled.

This wasn't going to be easy. Buell could be stubborn as a mule when he wanted to be. He would never do what she wanted if he thought she was trying to boss him. She took a deep breath to calm herself. "Your pigeons got canker," she said.

"They got what?"

"Canker. That's why they're so puny and don't hardly move around. What do you feed 'em?"

"Corn," he said. "What of it?"

"Animals are like people," Pam said. "They need all kinds of food to be healthy. I give my birds a mix—peas, seeds, grain. They love oats, but barley's better for 'em."

Buell laughed. "Sister, *we* don't eat that good."

It was hopeless. How could she get through to him when he wouldn't take her seriously? In desperation she blurted out, "They're going to all keel over and die if you don't—"

"Buell Leon Suggs!" It was Mattie. "Ma'll have your hide for smoking!"

"And she'll have yours for leaving the twins and sneaking out here to spy on me," Buell shot back.

Mattie's voice was self-righteous. "Ma sent me out here, Mr. Smarty-britches. To fetch Pam. Her ma's ready to leave."

Pam stared at the two of them. Between their bickering and Buell's stubbornness, it was clear she was wasting her time. She fled.

The next morning Pam was later than usual getting to school. Four o'clock had come awfully early. She couldn't

seem to drag herself out of bed after missing so much
sleep the previous night sitting up with Lula. All the way
from the steamer dock Pam could see Nina waiting for her
at the school yard fence.

She kept waving her arms for Pam to hurry, but Pam
was dreading school, and her feet felt like wooden stumps.
By the time Pam reached the school yard, Miss Merrell
was ringing the bell.

By then Nina was near to bursting. "That stranger
come to the schoolhouse yesterday! He asked Miss Merrell
where you were."

Questions were written all over Nina's face, but there
was no time for Pam to answer. "Tell you about it at recess,"
she promised Nina.

Talking alone with Nina at recess proved to be impos-
sible. The Currituck children swarmed around Pam,
buzzing about the German spy. Even the boys, who nor-
mally wouldn't budge from their baseball game to talk to
girls, were full of questions.

"What business did he have with you, Pam?"

"Never mind that. I wanna know what business he's
got in Currituck."

"Maybe the Germans are planning an invasion. My pa
said he's probably off a U-boat that's scouting Currituck
waters."

"Mama come home yesterday from her circle meeting
saying folks was talking about Germans putting broken

glass in Red Cross bandages. That true, Pam?"

Pam was starting to feel squeezed like an apple in a press. She was glad everyone had forgotten about the spelling lesson, but she felt uncomfortable talking to them about Arminger, especially since uneasiness was gnawing at her insides. Why was the stranger so eager to get ahold of her pigeons?

Trying to hold her anxiety in check, she answered coolly. "All I know is what he told me. He's settling in Currituck and wants to raise pigeons. He came out Monday evening to see mine. That's it."

"'That's it,' she says." Henry Bagley was holding the rolled tobacco twine the boys used for a ball. He tossed it in the air and caught it. Once. Twice. "But I have a question." He paused for effect, tossing the ball again. "Why would the spy want to buy Pam's stinky old birds?"

Pam's heartbeat quickened. How did Henry know about Arminger's offer? And now he had blurted it out to everyone in school. That bothered her immensely, though she wasn't sure why.

"My business ain't none of yours, Henry Bagley," she countered. No one would've guessed that her stomach was churning.

"That's okay," he said. "I can answer my own question. I can *imagine* why the spy visited your pigeons. Maybe"— he leered at Pam—"the man wanted pigeon stew."

Some of the boys laughed.

"Don't listen to him," Nina whispered fiercely.

Pam bit her tongue. Henry was goading her. She had promised Mama she wouldn't let him rile her anymore. Ignore him, Mama had told her. Which sounded easy beside the fire in the front room at home but wasn't so easy in front of every kid in Currituck.

Henry narrowed his eyes. "Or maybe . . ."—he drew the word out—"maybe . . . he came out to visit because of your pa."

A knot jerked itself tight in Pam's chest. Did Henry also know something about Papa, something she didn't know? Careful to hold her voice steady, she said, "What about Papa?"

"I know some things about him. Suspicious things."

Pam eyed Henry. She was willing to bet he was bluffing. If Henry really knew something, with his love for center stage, he'd waste no time in sharing it with everyone. "I don't think you know anything," she said.

"I know his letters come cut full of holes."

Relief washed over her. This was Henry's big news. "His letters are censored, you dunce. The army cuts out names of towns or anything that might give away where troops are moving. What're you looking at his letters for, anyway?"

"Hear that?" he said, ignoring her question. "She's calling *me* a dunce. Bet she can't even spell the word." He laughed.

Pam felt her face color. Her temples pounded. Fury mounted in her chest. If she opened her mouth to speak, she knew she would explode. She stood glaring at Henry.

He smirked back at her. "Wouldn't surprise me none if your pa was a spy too."

Henry had pushed Pam too far. Something inside of her snapped. "I'll give you a surprise, Henry Bagley!" Fists clenched, she swung at him. Her knuckles slammed into his chin, and he reeled backward, lost his balance, and fell. Pam was shaking all over. She couldn't believe she had really hit Henry. She hoped it would be over, that he wouldn't fight back, and for a long minute, she thought it was. He seemed stunned by her nerve; he lay on the ground, staring in disbelief. Then somebody snickered— she thought it was Sam—and Henry's eyes suddenly turned angry. He leaped to his feet and shoved Pam hard. She shoved him back. The next thing she knew they were rolling on the ground, tussling.

Then Miss Merrell was pulling her off of Henry. Miss Merrell's eyes flashed. "I'm ashamed of both of you." To the other children she said. "All of you. Inside now."

She grasped one of Pam's arms and one of Henry's, but her eyes, hard as stones, were riveted on Pam. "Henry's behavior doesn't surprise me. But you, Pam, what's gotten into you? Fighting like a boy. What do I have to do to get you to behave?"

Pam's face burned with shame. Why did she let Henry

get to her? Why couldn't she learn to rein her temper in?
There was no excuse for losing control, no excuse. She
wanted to beg Miss Merrell to forgive her, but her tongue
was cotton in her mouth; it wouldn't move. All she could
do was shake her head.

Pam's palms smarted where Miss Merrell had switched
them, but inside she felt numb. Being sent home early was
worse than staying after school; she had to bear everyone
staring at her as she walked down the aisle between desks
to the cloakroom. *They're all feeling sorry for me,* she
thought. She wanted to run out, like Henry had done, but
she made herself take slow, steady steps and hold her head
high. Pam had disgraced herself again—twice in less than
a week. What would Mama say this time?

Henry was waiting for her outside. "My pa's gonna fire
your mother when he hears what you did," he yelled. Then
he sprinted across the school yard and leaped over the
fence. Pam watched him disappear around the corner of
the red brick courthouse. Everyone in the drugstore would
know about her crime in a matter of minutes. Would Mr.
Bagley really fire Mama? How would they survive with no
money coming in? Would she be forced, after all, to make
a deal with Arminger?

She dragged along toward the drugstore, wrapped in

gloom, until she noticed a crowd milling around in front
of Purdy's Grain and Seed. Crowds in Currituck usually
meant news. When President Wilson asked Congress to
enter the war already raging in Europe, a special-edition
Gazette came by steamboat from Norfolk and half the town
gathered to hear Mr. Bagley read it out loud. It had been a
Saturday, and Pam was in town with Papa getting groceries.
Pam hadn't paid much mind to all the stir; Europe was
too far away from Currituck for her to care. Then like a
twister the war had yanked Papa clean away and set him
down way across the ocean right in the middle of it all.

Maybe something important had happened now,
something that had to do with the war. Pam hurried across
the street to see what the commotion was.

"What's going on?" she asked Mr. Connor Eagles, who
was standing at the back of the crowd. Mr. Connor was
over seventy and had a wooden leg, his own lost in "The
War," meaning the War for Southern Independence; to his
mind, there'd been no other war since.

"Folks is gawking at the motor truck. Seems to be no
end o' such newfangled contraptions. You wanna have a
look-see, li'l missy?" Mr. Connor was hard of hearing, half
blind, and had long since given up on trying to put names
with faces. He pushed Pam to the front of the crowd. "Let
this li'l gal get up there and see that foreigner's motor
truck."

Foreigner! This was Arminger's truck! Pam's pulse

pounded. Her eyes darted through the crowd, but she saw
no sign of the mysterious stranger. She couldn't help gawking, like everyone else. The truck was huge. It looked like
a farm wagon hitched to a locomotive. People were touch-
ing it timidly as if they thought it might bare its teeth at
any moment and bite. Though Pam had never seen a real
motor truck, she was more interested in its cargo than in
the machine. Dozens of sacks of grain were stacked in the
bed of the truck. What did Arminger plan to do with so
much grain?

Pam was craning her neck to try to make out the
printing on the sacks when she saw Arminger come out
of the Grain and Seed with another sack slung over his
shoulder. He looked right at her and grinned. He had
seen her!

Into Pam's mind flashed memories of the whispered
rumors, of Arminger's strange behavior, of Mama's warn-
ings. Sudden panic gripped her. She had to get away! She
turned and slipped back through the crowd. She heard
him behind her, pushing through the press of people. He
was coming after her! "Excuse me, madam. Excuse me."
His s's hissed, and Pam had an image of the serpent in
the Garden of Eden tempting Eve: "Did God ssssay . . ."
A needle-sharp fear twisted inside her.

Pam dived through the nearest doorway, which happened to be the dry goods store. Had Arminger seen her
go in? She winced as a bell above the door tinkled,

announcing her entry to the owner, Mr. Dozier . . . and to Arminger. Quickly she ducked behind some bolts of cloth standing upright on a rear counter.

Mr. Dozier had his back turned, stocking shelves, and didn't bother turning around. He was known for his lack-adaisical attitude toward customers. "Can I help you?" Pam heard him mutter. There was no way he could see her way back here, but she hunkered lower behind the counter. She willed her heartbeat to slow down, sure its hammering would give her away. A cold sweat ran down her neck.

Finally she heard, "Dang wind." Mr. Dozier thought the door had been blown open by the wind! She figured that meant she was safe . . . for now. She slumped to the floor and tried to think what to do next. She couldn't stay put; it was only a matter of time before Mr. Dozier or a browsing customer wandered back and found her. There had to be a back door somewhere. But where?

Then she jumped half out of her skin as a voice above her head whispered, "Playing hooky, Pam?"

Pam looked up into the smiling face of Miss Sadie Ritch, the seamstress. Miss Sadie was an old maid, nearly thirty and unmarried, but she gave the girls scraps of fabric to use for doll dresses, and Pam liked her. Only thing about Miss Sadie, she could talk the ear off a mule. She might hold Pam here till kingdom come asking questions, and any minute Arminger could come barging through the

door after her. Pam had to cut loose from Miss Sadie and
get out of here somehow—and fast.

"Hey there, Miss Sadie," Pam murmured, her eyes
flicking from Miss Sadie's face to the door and back. "I
was hunting for . . . Mama promised me a new ribbon for
my Sunday hat." That was the truth, though not the
answer Miss Sadie had been looking for. Which made it as
good as a lie, Pam thought guiltily. She squirmed. Miss
Sadie looked doubtful. A bigger lie helped itself out of
Pam's mouth. "Just came over for recess," she stammered.
"Gotta go now . . . get back to school." Pam was disgusted
with the ease of her fibbing.

Pam's self-reproach turned to alarm as the bell above
the door tinkled. "You know Pam Lowder, yah?" It was
Arminger! Talking to Mr. Dozier!

Every muscle in Pam's body tensed. She lifted a finger
to her lips and looked at Miss Sadie. *Don't give me away,*
she silently pleaded.

Miss Sadie crouched beside Pam and whispered,
"That's him? The one they say is a German?" Her eyes
were alive with interest. "What on earth does he want
with you, child?"

Pam's words were barely audible and filled with fear.
"I don't know, Miss Sadie. I don't know."

Miss Sadie glanced to the front of the store. She
seemed to be studying a rack of ready-made shirts in the
aisle. Pam could hear Mr. Dozier talking, then Arminger.

"I saw her come in here," Arminger was saying.

Suddenly Miss Sadie snapped her eyes back to Pam. "Come." She pulled Pam into the storage room adjoining the store and pointed to a door that stood open to the breeze. "Through there, child. Run."

Pam ran.

CHAPTER 5
A PROWLER

Pam took a roundabout route through town, running all the way. She didn't feel safe until she reached the drugstore and there was still no sign of Arminger.

She collapsed on the front steps, gasping for breath. It was only then she remembered her disgrace at school and Henry's threat to have Mama fired.

She picked herself up and made herself go into the store. Mama was wiping down the glass doors of the big oak cabinet where Mr. Bagley displayed his wares. On the top shelf were the ladies' toiletries: jars of cold cream, hairbrushes and combs, nail files, bath powder, fans. Under that were shaving mugs for the men and boxes of cigars and pipe tobacco, and the bottom shelf held soap flakes and toothpaste. On the other side of the cabinet were the tonics and cure-alls: Rexall Olive Oil Emulsion, Rexall Liver Salts, Gold Medal Ephedrine Nasal Jelly,

Dr. Miles' Laxative Cold Cure, Karnac Stomachic Tonic and System Regulator.

At least Mama still has her job, thought Pam with relief. Mr. Bagley was nowhere in sight.

"Has Henry been here?" Pam asked Mama.

"He ran in a while ago, but skedaddled when he found out his pa had gone out to Slidell. We sold clean out of all those bottles of old Mr. Tripp's nerve tonic, and Mr. Bagley went to fetch some more," Mama said. "What you two doing out of school?"

Pam poured the whole story out to Mama, including the episode with Mr. Arminger. She left out only the part about Henry's threat. There was no use worrying Mama since Henry hadn't carried through yet. Mama listened without saying much, but Pam could tell she was none too pleased with any of it. When Pam finished, Mama was silent for a minute. "Well, I hope you're pure ashamed of yourself."

Pam hung her head. "Yes, ma'am. Terrible."

"That's punishment enough then. 'Cept maybe you're due to copy down some Bible verses 'bout patience and not being provoked to wrath. You got to learn to put up with Henry, Pam. Ain't no two ways about it."

Pam knew Mama was right. But she still wondered how Henry could have known Arminger wanted to buy her pigeons. She asked Mama.

"Why, Henry was here the whole time I was talking

with Mr. Arminger, the first time he came in asking after
your pigeons. Henry run over from the schoolhouse during
recess. He was up at the soda fountain, begging his pa for
Coca-Cola, but I s'pose he could've heard most of what
was said."

Mama stopped her cleaning and looked earnestly at
Pam. "Listen, honey. About Mr. Arminger. I'm afraid I
scared you the other evening. Ain't no cause to fret if he
speaks to you first. Just don't be over-friendly till we know
him better, hear?"

Pam nodded. "What about all the talk about him?"

Mama chuckled. "Funny how quick that German spy
business settled down once he commenced to spending
good American dollars. Miz Langley flounced in here this
morning singing a total opposite tune. Said Mr. Arminger
gave an in-spirin' address at the community loyalty meeting last night *and* a heap of money to her Red Cross goose
sale. Now she's plumb tickled he's settling down in
Currituck."

"He's staying then?"

"Already bought him up a piece of land in the woods
upcreek from us," Mama said. "You recollect old Sanders
the hermit? Your papa used to fish and hunt with him
years ago. Papa was pretty much the only person Sanders
would cotton to, and it was Papa who found him dead in
his cabin and buried him, remember?"

"Yes, ma'am, I do. Papa took me out to his cabin a few

times. Mr. Sanders kept a passel of animals in the house.
His coon ate out of my hand, but wouldn't get near Papa.
Mr. Sanders said he could tell I had a rare way with animals."

Mama nodded, remembering. "Seems Mr. Arminger is
setting up housekeeping in Sanders' old cabin. The way I
hear it, he's a fisherman from New England, come south
with his sons to take up herring fishing. And he's looking
to raise some birds, he says, leghorn chickens maybe.
Maybe pigeons."

At that moment suspicion flared in the pit of Pam's
stomach. Arminger's story didn't add up. "He didn't appear
to know a thing about fishing the other night. Seemed to
know more about animals than anything else."

"He's been fishing up north, sugar. I reckon it's a
different business up there."

"Don't it seem peculiar he was buying grain instead of
fishing gear?"

"Likely he already has his gear."

"But, Mama, all that grain—like he already had him a
mess of pigeons."

Mama heaved an impatient sigh. "Pam, leave it be. The
man prob'ly up and bought birds from someone else. Yours
ain't the only pigeons in the county."

Pam fell silent. She was deeply stung. She hadn't realized how much Arminger's admiration had meant to her.
Now he appeared to have found other pigeons that suited
him. A passel of 'em.

The wind was blowing steady out of the northeast by the time Pam and Mama got home. Gray clouds hung low in the sky, and the creek was chopping straight up and down. It was prime fishing weather. Bluefish would be running; spotted sea trout would be up the river.

"Wouldn't Papa be rarin' to get out on the water?" said Pam aloud. She was on her way to the toolshed where she stored her pigeons' food. A voice inside her added, *If he was here.* Pam's throat swelled and ached. Nothing was the same with Papa gone. Nothing.

Then Bosporus came bounding out of nowhere, barking furiously. The wind was bristling his fur and making the hair on his neck stand straight up. He jumped up on Pam and seemed to dance for a minute on his hind legs. Pam laughed. He reminded her of a clown she'd seen once on a circus poster.

Pam stroked his muzzle affectionately. "You're in high spirits today. Can you feel the storm coming on?" Bosporus whined deep in his throat and loped to the toolshed. He stood outside the door whimpering.

"You are some anxious to get them pigeons fed, ain't ya, boy?" When she opened the shed door, though, she realized it wasn't high spirits that had Bosporus acting funny. Sacks of barley and oats lay askew, spilling their contents onto the floor. Maple peas and sunflower seeds were scattered everywhere. Some old feeding troughs had been knocked off a shelf. An empty paper sack, blown by the wind from the open window, scratched across the plank floor.

"So. This is what you were trying to tell me, Bos," Pam said with dismay. "Someone's been in here. Escaped through the window, looks like." She pushed down the sash with a bang. "Who was it, Bos? Someone you—" But she cut herself off. Something was moving down by the barn!

She raced outside. Daylight was fading fast. The bullfrogs from the creek were starting to growl, the crickets to sing. Had she really seen anything? Maybe it was just her imagination.

No, there it was again, a shadow flitting into the barn!

Her senses alert, Pam crept into the dimness of the barn. She held her breath, waiting, waiting to hear something, anything, out of the ordinary. But there was nothing. Only Lula and Daisy stamping in their stalls. Pyrenees lowing for milk. A mouse scuttling up in the hayloft. She searched the empty stalls, the corner behind the plow and the old wagon, the tack room where Papa kept his crab pots and fishing nets and his hip boots. Nothing.

Bosporus was lying obediently just outside the barn waiting for Pam. "I could've sworn I saw someone," she told him as she fastened the latch on the barn door. He whined and thumped his tail on the ground.

That was when Pam noticed the cigarette butt in the

dirt. "How did that get here?" She bent to pick it up, but suddenly froze. Her pigeons were squawking!

Padding as quietly as she could through the growing darkness, she hurried to the loft. The wind had picked up, and it was growing cold. All she could see were shapes and shadows, until she was nearly on top of the loft. Then what she saw sent a shiver down her spine.

It was Arminger. With Caspian perched on his shoulder.

CHAPTER 6

MAMA'S ULTIMATUM

What are you doing with my bird?" Pam demanded. Her voice trembled with anger. Caspian flapped off Arminger's shoulder and lighted on hers. Pam felt a rush of affection for her favorite pigeon. She stroked his silky crop with one finger.

"I came back to try to convince you to sell your birds," said Arminger. "They seemed agitated, and I found this one loose. Apparently he escaped through that hole in your fly-pen." He pointed to a gap in the mesh near the base of the fly-pen.

"How did that come loose?" Pam crouched to examine the hole. Too many fishy things had been happening lately—and they all seemed to happen when Arminger was around. "Looks like it was pried loose." Her voice held accusation—purposely.

Arminger made no comment, though Pam didn't see how he could have missed the meaning of her tone. She pushed the mesh down and secured it with a rock.

"Your bird"—Arminger nodded toward Caspian—"is very well trained. Responds to your voice, yah?"

Pam fought the warmth unfurling inside her. She would not be led on by Arminger's flattery. "My birds trust me," she said coldly, "and they know who feeds them."

"But surely there's something you do, techniques you use, a certain way of handling, that creates that trust." Arminger's voice was animated. "Night-flying pigeons. A dog learning not to be a dog. These are not ordinary animals you have here."

He flipped a hand toward Bosporus, standing at Pam's heels. A growl rumbled deep in Bosporus' throat. Pam scratched behind her dog's ears to calm him. A whip-poorwill sounded in the distance. Pam made no reply to Arminger.

He was not easily discouraged. "Your dog—Bos you call him—a cross of setter and wolf. A rare union, I would say. How did that come about?"

"I don't know, really. I found him in the woods a few months ago, hurt bad. He was just a wee thing, cussed as a snake, but he answered real fast to a little attention. And to Mama's good cooking." Pam felt herself warming to Arminger; she couldn't help it. She'd never known anyone else as passionate about animals as she was.

"Wasn't long before he was eating out of my hand," she went on. "Now he looks after my pigeons like they were his own pups." She hesitated a moment. Maybe she was giving Arminger the wrong impression about Bos. Her dog was no pansy. The man might think he could get away with something. "I wouldn't get too near him, though. He can be right hard on folks he don't cotton to."

"I understand. Otherwise he wouldn't be much use as a watchdog."

Pam marveled at the way Arminger echoed her own thoughts. Like he could read her mind. It was almost scary.

Arminger lit up a cigarette. "I still want your pigeons, Pam. Very badly. At least let me have one pair—that fine cock there, and his mate. I'll still give you the two hundred. For those birds alone."

Pam gasped. A hundred dollars a bird! If she sold her whole loft at that rate—"No!" she cried. She wouldn't even think about it. "Not Caspian. He's my favorite bird."

"Any pair then. Any of your best-trained birds." Arminger took a draw from his cigarette. Its orange end glowed in the darkness.

Something nagged at Pam's brain that she couldn't quite put her finger on. Something about Arminger. What was it?

He must have taken her hesitation for weakness. "Two hundred dollars would help your family a lot. Yah?"

Pam felt herself wavering. *Talks like buttermilk, he does, all rich and smooth.* If she let him go on, she'd end up selling. And be sorry later.

"I got to tend my birds now, Mr. Arminger," she said firmly. She started to walk away.

"Pam, I've got to have those pigeons." Arminger had always maintained a cool exterior. Now his voice sounded urgent. "If it's money, I can give you more. Cash, right now." He stepped toward Pam and reached into his pocket.

The next thing Pam knew, Bosporus was lunging at Arminger, snarling and barking. For one horrible moment Pam watched her dog's teeth sink into Arminger's leg. "No! Bosporus!" she shouted, and vaulted forward to pull him away. It was all she could do to hold her dog back as he continued to strain forward and bark at Arminger.

Mama appeared out of the darkness. "Pam! Are you all right?" She held the shotgun.

"Yes, ma'am, I'm fine." Pam couldn't keep her voice from shaking.

"It was my fault." Arminger sounded contrite. "I made a sudden movement toward Pam, and the dog took offense. I should've known better. It's not a serious bite. He got a mouthful of trousers more than anything."

"Pam?" Mama was politely asking if Arminger was telling the truth.

"That's right, Mama. He was trying to give me money for the pigeons, but I . . . I decided I don't want to sell them." Pam felt like crying. She wasn't sure now whether she had done the right thing. Would Mama be mad at her for turning down so much money?

"You're sure you're not hurt?" Mama asked Arminger.
He nodded. "Barely broke the skin."

"Then I think it's time you left." Mama's tone gave no
room for argument. "And I'd be obliged if you'd not bother
Pam anymore about her birds."

"No, you're right. I'll bother her no more. I do apolo-
gize for my behavior. Good night." He tipped his hat and
was gone.

Arminger's departure left Pam feeling relieved but
strangely empty. He had appreciated her skill with animals
like no one else ever had, except Papa. "Reckon he's gone
for good?" she said, to herself as much as Mama.

"I don't think he'll pester you no more. He seems right
decent after all." Her words were distracted, like she was
thinking about something else.

Pam sighed. Maybe it *was* for the best he was gone.
But there was still something about him that was nagging
at Pam. Something that bothered her, though she couldn't
pin it down.

Mama took Pam's cheeks in her palms. "There's something hard I got to say to you, sweetie." She paused. "Your
dog ain't a pup no more. He's growing so big . . ." Her
voice trailed off.

Pam went stiff. What was Mama getting at?

Then Mama spoke again, rushing the words. "Fact is,
Pam, he was born wild, and he's still wild. Ain't no amount
of gentling that's going to tame that streak out of 'im."

Pam felt a numbness mushroom through her body. She reached down and knit her fingers into Bosporus' thick fur. He was so warm. . . .

"We can't have him attacking innocent folks, Pam. What if he went for one of the Suggs younguns? I don't think it's going to work to keep him here on the farm."

Mama wanted her to get rid of Bosporus! The knowledge hit Pam like a hurricane. "No, Mama! He was only protecting me. And Caspian." Her own words seemed to shake her brain loose, and instantly she realized what had been nagging her about Arminger. The cigarette butt down at the barn—it was his! It had to be! It was proof that Arminger had been skulking around their property, up to no good.

Quickly Pam told Mama about her suspicions.

"Pam, a cigarette butt don't prove a thing. You don't know for a fact it was Mr. Arminger's. Remember, Buell came over for the crab pots this morning. His mama told me he's been smoking on the sly. Maybe the butt was Buell's. Was it homemade or store-bought?"

"I didn't look that close. There was all that commotion at the pigeon loft. . . ."

"I don't know, sugar. I think you're grasping at straws. And it still don't change the facts about your dog. He's got to go back to the woods, Pam. He knows how to fend for himself. Take him out a ways and turn him loose, first thing in the morning."

"What if he comes back?" Pam was hoping.

"Then next time make sure he don't, you hear me?" Mama's tone said the matter was closed. "See to your chores now, and come on in the house for some supper."

Pam let her pigeons out for exercise. Then she milked Daisy and went back to feed her pigeons and lock them up for the night. Bosporus didn't leave her side for a minute, as if he knew something was amiss.

While Pam fixed the hole in the fly-pen, she explained to him that he couldn't linger around the farm anymore. "But I'll come visit you in the woods and take you squirrel hunting with me. How's that?" He thumped his tail and opened his mouth in what looked like a grin. Pam swallowed a lump in her throat. Maybe Bosporus would be happier in the woods than he was on the farm. For his sake, she hoped so.

With a heavy heart she told him it was his last night under the barn. "Better hunker in tight," she said. "A nor'easter's beginning to blow."

All night the storm raged. The morning was gray and mean, with a steady downpour and a wind that bored holes through Pam's slicker. Head down, she fought through the rain to the pigeon loft to care for her birds. Homers could fly in the rain, but Pam would never let them out even in the fly-pen in a wind this strong. They would have to be content with flapping about inside the loft for today.

Pam closed her eyes against the biting wind. The rain stung her face, but she was glad of it for one reason: Mama had postponed Bosporus' exile until tomorrow. She wished there was some way she could convince Mama to let him stay. This was all Arminger's fault, she thought angrily. She wished he had never set foot in Currituck.

She fumbled blindly for the latch on the loft door, but her wet fingers kept slipping. She opened her eyes to a slit in order to grasp the latch.

What she saw made her stomach turn.

Two black feathers floated on top of a puddle. Two black feathers from one of her pigeons.

CHAPTER 7
STOLEN BIRDS

A strangled cry escaped from Pam's throat. Something had happened to Orleans, her second-best cock! He was the only bird she had that was solid black.

Pam's fear was confirmed inside the loft. Orleans was gone. Little Verdun, usually saucy with snapping, bright eyes, sat alone in the nest box with her wings drooping. She missed her mate.

Pam felt sick. It was clear what had happened. Since she had refused to sell Arminger any pigeons, he had decided to up and take one. But why had he stolen only Orleans and not Verdun? A cock wouldn't do him much good without a hen. Unless he planned to mate Orleans with a bird of his own.

Angry thoughts whirled through Pam's head. She'd known from the start Arminger wasn't to be trusted; she'd had a funny feeling about him all along. All that money, the man thought he could do as he pleased. Well, he wouldn't get away with stealing her pigeon. She wouldn't let him. All she needed was proof. Proof that he had been lurking about on the farm, waiting for a chance to make his move.

The only proof she had was that cigarette butt down by the barn.

Pam searched all over for the butt, but she knew it was pointless. The storm had washed away every trace.

Pam poured out her thoughts to Mama on the walk into town that morning. The weather was far too rough to risk taking the skiff. Mama felt bad for Pam, but she said there was no way they could prove Arminger had stolen Orleans. "Maybe Orleans somehow escaped on his own," she suggested.

Any pigeoneer would know better, Pam thought fiercely. No homer would venture out in a storm like that on its own. But she didn't dare say that to Mama. Mama would call it impudence.

By the time Pam got to school, it was past recess. She had missed spelling, thank goodness, but she had also missed half the arithmetic lesson. Now she would never get the hang of fractions. Never. At least Henry wasn't there to torment her today. Maybe he had caught the grippe and would be sick in bed for days. Or weeks. Mama would scold her for wishing him ill, but Pam couldn't help it. If anybody deserved the grippe, it was Henry.

The rain stopped about the time school got out, but the sky, gray as shingles, promised more later. Pam walked Nina home and told her all about Arminger and the stolen pigeon. Nina agreed entirely with Pam, as usual.

"Of course he did it, Pam," said Nina matter-of-factly. "He's a German. What d'you expect?"

"Well, no one knows *for sure* he's a German," Pam said. She wasn't sure why she felt obligated to offer that defense, especially for a rat like Arminger. "But he sure does act like one," she threw in quickly.

"Look, Pam." Nina pointed to the sawmill down by the riverbank. "Speak of the devil. Or devils." Arminger and two other men Pam didn't know were loading his truck with lumber. And there was Henry, lolling around the truck, his jaw pumping up and down like he was talking their ears off.

"What's Henry doing over there?" Nina said.

"Probably pestering 'em to death. Good! Arminger deserves Henry!" There was bitterness in Pam's voice.

"Wonder why Henry wasn't in school today," Nina said.

"I don't care. He can play hooky every day if he wants to. The less I see of Henry Bagley, the better."

Pam left Nina at her gate and went on alone to the drugstore. Alice Bagley and Louisa White were sitting on the front steps of the store, sipping lemonade from tall glasses.

"Hey, Pam," said Alice. "I been dying to talk to you all day."

"Yeah? You saw me at school," said Pam, a little irked. Alice was always too busy with her friends to speak to Pam at school.

"Well, you were talking to Nina and all." Alice pursed her lips and sipped from the glass. "I thought you'd want to know Henry got it from Pa last night for picking a fight with you. Henry tried to make out like you started it all, but *I* told Pa what really happened."

"Oh." Pam stumbled for something appropriate to say. Maybe Alice was trying to be nice, but she always made Pam feel like a charity case. Alice's face said she expected to be thanked, but Pam couldn't push gracious words off her tongue. Her pride wouldn't let her. "That's good, Alice" was the best she could manage. Pam chewed nervously on the inside of her lip, while an awkward silence stretched between them.

Finally Alice broke it. "Just keep an eye on him. He's hopping mad."

"Says he's going to get even with you," Louisa added dramatically.

Pam's temper flared. When would Henry Bagley leave

her be? "Tell him I'm quaking like a rabbit." She marched past them and up the steps, seething. That Henry was worse than a redbug for getting under her skin. She took a deep breath to calm herself before she went into the store. It wouldn't do for Mama to see her so riled over Henry again.

Pam didn't mention a thing about Henry to Mama, but she did tell Mama she saw Arminger loading up his truck with lumber.

"Oh, yeah," said Mama. "We been hearing all morning about how much money that man is spending. Wonder where he gets it from, in these times." Mama was at the cash register, counting the day's receipts.

"Don't know 'bout that, but word is he's fixing up old man Sanders' place. Which sets tongues wagging even faster." Mr. Bagley's voice boomed from the back room where he mixed prescriptions. Pam could see him through the service window, pouring liquids into a medicine glass. He stirred the concoction, poured it into a bottle, and brought it to the cash register where Mama was closing out the drawer. "For Luther Truitt when he comes in tomorrow morning. His boy's got the croup," Mr. Bagley said to Mama. Then he looked at Pam and winked. "Sanders was a sorcerer, y'know. Minnie Midyette swears old Sanders hexed her pa's fishing nets and put him out of business."

Mama snorted. "Merl Midyette put himself out of business by sleeping till noon every day."

"Still," said Mr. Bagley, "folks been scared of that old place ever since Sanders passed on. It's haunted, they say, and Arminger's asking for trouble by moving in there."

A clap of thunder startled Pam; rain suddenly pounded on the roof. The front door slammed, and Alice and Louisa dashed in with water streaming down their faces and dripping off their frilly white dresses. With their bobs pasted flat to their heads, they looked bald as newborn possums. Pam tried hard to suppress a giggle. Mr. Bagley laughed out loud.

"Pa, it's not funny," Alice whined. "My new dress is ruined."

"Sears-Roebuck dries just like homemade, my dear," said Mr. Bagley. "Ain't no sense in having clothes too fancy for Currituck weather. You girls seen Henry? I want him to tote Miz Lowder and Pam home in the buggy."

Pam groaned inwardly. Given a choice between swimming in a riptide and riding home with Henry, Pam thought she would choose the riptide.

Henry was far worse than the riptide, Pam decided. The boy bragged for a solid hour, all the way home. Mama sat up front with him, saying "Ain't that something" and "I know your ma and pa are real proud of you, Henry." Pam sat in back, rolling her eyes and wondering how long a body could go on about one blessed picture show he saw in Norfolk.

The rain had slowed to a steady drizzle that robbed the landscape of its fall brilliance. The rich red of the sumacs and maples was dulled to the color of old bricks, and the yellows of the willow and black cherry trees were a washed-out beige. Pam felt listless and depressed. The buggy ride seemed endless. Finally she saw the wind-twisted cedar that stood watch at the edge of their property.

But Henry wasn't about to shut up. "I reckon you know I been made head of the Boys' Relief Corps, Miz Lowder."

"Yes, Henry, I do recollect you mentioning something about that," said Mama.

"That's 'cause he's mentioned it about five times," retorted Pam. Mama's scorching look in her direction kept Pam from adding *and that's only today.* Great goodness, Pam told herself, you'd think Henry would catch on that everyone knew he was only appointed because his father was Red Cross director. But no, he would go on and on as if he was a flying ace shooting down German airplanes.

"I'm in charge of putting all the boys in town to work raising fall gardens to help out the war effort." Henry, still boasting, drove the buggy up under the grove of live oaks in the Lowders' front yard. Beneath the canopy of leaves and Spanish moss, the ground was barely wet.

Pam scrambled out of the buggy before the wheels stopped turning. She thought she would be sick if she had to listen to Henry any longer. She caught hold of the horse's bridle, caressing its velvety muzzle to calm herself. She had always wanted a horse, but all they'd ever had was old Trixie the mule. Trixie had up and died this past summer, and Mama said there wasn't money nor reason to replace her; they'd not be plowing with Papa gone, and it was faster to row into town than to take the wagon, anyway. Pam missed Trixie, even if she was the stubbornest thing this side of the Currituck River.

"I reckon you got your hands full, Henry," Mama said as she climbed out of the buggy. "Hope you'll still be able to come help us out on Saturday."

"That's just it. I can't come Saturday. I got to go 'round and get some of the boys started on their gardens," Henry said. "But Pa says I got to come out to your place sometime, so he said to skip church Sunday and come. Ma says it's okay since it's our Christian duty to help out those less fortunate than us."

Pam's temper shot sky-high. She'd give Henry Bigmouth a Christian duty! It wasn't like they had ever asked for his help, and as far as Pam was concerned, they'd be better off without it. She couldn't believe Henry would dare smart off like that to Mama. She rubbed the horse's cheek with long, firm strokes, waiting for Mama to deliver Henry's tongue-lashing.

But instead of giving Henry what-for, Mama thanked him—*thanked him!* "We'll expect you for Sunday dinner then," she said, as if Henry had tipped his hat instead of insulted them.

Pam seethed. Mama and her southern courtesy! If Pam had things her way, she'd teach Henry a thing or two about courtesy, she sure would. Furiously she stroked the horse's neck.

Then Henry had the gall to ask what they were having for dinner. "Corned ham? I love it stuck full of cloves," he said with longing.

Pam couldn't contain her temper a minute longer. "You know good and well we gave up eating ham for the war effort!" The horse stamped its foot and whinnied.

"Now, Pam," said Mama evenly. "Henry likely don't know we pledged to give up pork entirely, 'stead of just on Thursdays and Saturdays like the government asked. I'll stew a chicken, Henry, and make persimmon pudding. How's that?"

"Yes'm, that sounds mighty good." Henry was getting down from the buggy. He planned to stay! Well, he had another think coming if he planned to tag along with Pam. She was so mad right now she felt like she would bust wide open. "I'll be down at my loft, Mama," she said through clenched teeth.

"Hold on," said Henry, "I'm coming, too. I ain't seen your pigeons in a while—not since they got famous. Hah." His voice was mocking.

Pam's stomach quivered like a sack full of hornets. She

glared at Henry, her lips trembling with angry words she couldn't say. She whirled and stalked down the slope to the loft. The cold drizzle raised goose pimples on her arms. Behind her, Henry's boots thudded in the sand, and she picked up her pace. Maybe she couldn't stop him from following her, but she could make it clear he wasn't welcome.

The loft looked forlorn in the gray mist. Pam noticed the whitewash had faded and the roof sagged a little on one side. Papa had always prided himself on keeping their outbuildings in fine shape. *Papa's not here anymore,* an inner voice murmured. A sense of gloom overwhelmed her, and she rushed into the loft before Henry could see the tears welling up in her eyes.

A soft *groo-groo* greeted Pam inside. A few birds whirred from their perches to the floor, anticipating dinner. The sounds of her pigeons were gentle and soothing. She felt the tension slowly drain from her muscles.

Then Henry burst through the door, and the pigeons set up a frenzied din. "It smells in here," he announced loudly.

But his comment didn't register with Pam. She was too intent on frantically searching every nest box in the loft.

Another pigeon was missing. And this time it was Caspian.

CHAPTER 8
PAM'S PLAN

Anguish ripped through Pam. Caspian gone! Arminger had stolen the one bird that he knew was most special to her.

Inhuman, said a voice inside her head, echoing Mr. Bagley's pronouncement about the Germans in Belgium. This proved Arminger was German, if anything did. The word formed itself on her lips and escaped as a rasping whisper. "Inhuman."

"Huh?" said Henry. "What do you mean, 'inhuman'?" His eyes held a spark of interest.

Numbness was closing in on Pam. She shook her head. She tried to push her voice from her throat. It came out husky. "A pigeon's missing. My best one."

"Is that all?" The spark in his eyes died. "It's one stupid bird. You've got a whole shed full. What are you worried about?"

Pam's anger came alive. "Caspian ain't just any pigeon,"

she snapped. "Breeding and training first-rate homers takes years." A fire had ignited inside her, and she couldn't stop herself from going on. "That bird"—she mocked Henry's tone—"is worth a hundred dollars. That's what the German was going to give me for him." She couldn't bring herself to say Arminger's name.

Henry stared at Pam with disbelief. "You're lying," he said. "If the spy offered you that much money, as poor as your family is, you'd have took it. Your ma would've made you."

The fire in Pam's belly blazed higher. "These birds are mine, Henry Bagley, and I do with 'em whatever I want." Pam held her voice low to avoid scaring the birds, but she let her eyes spit out the fury she felt. She wanted Henry out of her sight before she lost control. She planted her hands on her hips and spoke, emphasizing each word. "Get out of my loft and off our land. Before I sic my dog on you." Her expression dared Henry to do anything else.

For endless seconds Henry stood his ground, glaring at her. The pigeons felt the tension and set up a fretful chatter. Outwardly Pam didn't move; inwardly her mind raced. What would she do if Henry called her bluff? Bos would answer her call in a flash, but if she sicced him on Henry, Mama would be fit to be tied. No telling what fate would then be ordered for her dog. Pam berated herself for tacking the threat onto her demand. She glared back at Henry, furious that he had backed her into this corner.

Finally Henry spoke. "Like I said, this place smells. But it's not the birds." He turned and stomped out of the loft.

Pam held her breath until the sound of his footsteps died. Then she slowly released the air from her lungs. With it, every ounce of strength seemed to drain from her body. She slumped to the floor and let the birds hop into her lap and perch on her head. Their cooing was rich and throaty, a pigeon melody. It reminded Pam of the spirituals Mama used to sing to put her to sleep: "Way Down upon the Swanee River" and "Swing Low, Sweet Chariot." A deep sadness yawned inside her. If only she could stay here in the loft forever and never have to move. . . .

Caspian's little hen Odessa flew from her nest box and lighted on the floor beside Pam. Pam lifted a finger and stroked the bird's fluffy crown. Odessa puffed her neck feathers and scolded loudly, as if she blamed Pam for the disappearance of her mate.

That broke Pam's heart. She couldn't bear to stay in the loft and listen to Odessa accuse her. The pigeons fluttered off her as she rose heavily from the floor. Her body felt like a millstone. Mechanically she walked to the door, opened it, and went outside. It was still raining.

She headed to the barn. Across the cow lot, she saw Bosporus standing under a magnolia tree, watching her. He seemed to know he was no longer welcome on the farm. His huge, brindled head was bent against the rain, and his tail hung low.

Pam's emotions went out to him. She whistled.

Bosporus' head snapped up. He bounded toward her through the swampy cow lot and leaped over the barbwire fence, landing in a puddle the size of the Atlantic Ocean. He struggled in the quagmire for a minute before pulling himself out and shaking his coat, in the process spraying Pam with big globs of mud. Then he planted his muddy, oversized paws on her chest and yipped happily.

Pam couldn't help laughing, even though her insides ached. She was losing everything she cared about. First Papa, then her favorite pigeons, soon Bosporus. What next, she wondered, what next?

She wrapped her arms around her dog's neck. "I can't send you away now," she said. "Not this evening. I need a friend. You can stay inside the barn just this once, huh? Mama won't know. I'll get you out in the morning before she sees you."

It wasn't easy coaxing Bos into the barn; he knew he wasn't supposed to go through those doors. Pam finally had to drag him in, while her conscience screamed at her. Not only was she defying Mama's orders, she was betraying the careful training she had given her dog. How could he be anything but confused once she had forced him to disobey the very rule she had taught him?

She could hear Papa lecturing her about consistency with her animals. A well-trained animal, Papa had drilled into her, would give one hundred percent as long as he

knew what was expected of him. "Howsomever," Papa
would say, "once them expectations get fuzzy in a critter's
head, he turns to being unpredictable, and he's ruint for
further useful purpose." Then he would look at her sternly
and say, "Don't you ever forget that, Pammie."

She never had forgotten it, until now. *But you didn't
really forget,* her conscience told her. *You just chose to ignore
what your papa said.*

The accusation stung her, but she knew it was true. Her
world seemed to be falling apart, and it was all because
Papa had left them, gone to fight in some crazy, faraway
war that wouldn't change a thing in Currituck, win or lose.
If Papa had been here, Arminger wouldn't have dared to
steal her pigeons. That she knew.

But facts were facts. Papa *wasn't* here, and Arminger
had stolen her pigeons. Now she had to figure out what to
do about it. She sighed heavily and sank to the floor of the
empty stall. Bosporus sprawled beside her.

Mama had made it clear that she wouldn't call the law
on Arminger unless Pam had some proof that he was
guilty. What Pam needed was evidence, evidence that
pointed to Arminger.

She wracked her brain, going over and over every
detail of every conversation she had had with him. But she
couldn't find a single action or word that positively
incriminated him. There was only the way she had felt
about him, uncomfortable, like he wasn't quite leveling

with her. There were the little things that didn't add up in his story. A fisherman who knew more about pigeons than about fishing. A truck full of grain for a "few birds." An obsession with getting her pigeons at any price.

Arminger was a sly one, all right. He threw money around town to foster Currituck's goodwill, but no one really knew anything about him. He acted suspiciously, but he never lied outright, at least not a lie that anyone had caught him in. He took her pigeons and slipped away without a trace, knowing full well that a little girl could never prove he was the thief.

The more Pam thought about it, the madder she got. She *would* prove it! See if she wouldn't!

A plan began to take shape in her mind. So Arminger was fitting out Sanders' old cabin to set up housekeeping with his sons. Why had he chosen such a desolate piece of land to buy, in the middle of a cypress swamp? A mighty strange place for a herring fisherman to live. It seemed peculiar to Pam that none of the grown-ups had asked themselves that question. Pam figured they were too busy counting Arminger's money to mind about such a little detail.

Then suddenly the perfect nature of Arminger's setup hit her. Yessirree, a cypress swamp was a strange place to fish for herring. But it was a mighty fine place to hide stolen pigeons. And if everyone thought the place was haunted, no one would ever come to visit and find the pigeons, or anything else he had hidden there, would they?

Pam clucked. Arminger must be feeling right cocky about pulling everything off as pretty as you please. *Not for long,* she thought. A plan had laid itself out in her mind like a map. "I'm going out there," she told Bosporus. "Tomorrow. I'll go into town with Mama, like I'm bound for school. I'll tell her not to wait for me after, 'cause I'm going to Nina's and her father'll tote me home. After I drop Mama off, I'll hightail it back here and get the canoe me and Papa made. Then I'll paddle out to Sanders' place and find my pigeons. It's that simple."

Bosporus looked at her with bright eyes and lolled his tongue out of his mouth. *I have complete confidence in you,* he seemed to be saying.

"Thanks, boy," she said, scratching behind his ear. If only she had so much confidence in herself.

CHAPTER 9
INTO THE SWAMP

The walk home from town the next morning seemed like nothing to Pam, though it was over six miles. She was in high spirits. At last she was doing something about Arminger, rather than sitting idly by while he helped himself to her pigeons one by one.

A chalky sky threatened more rain, but some sun managed to filter through the clouds, and the air smelled new. The soggy fields teemed with birds: flocks of grackles, killdeers with their mournful *kill-dee, kill-dee,* bobolinks and meadowlarks crooning.

At home Pam grabbed a cold sweet potato and a couple of biscuits from the kitchen to eat later. She carried her belt hatchet and pocketknife as she always did when she went into the woods. Best to be prepared, Papa always said. From a shelf in the shed she pulled down one of the special baskets Papa made for carrying pigeons on his fishing boat. Inside the baskets were little hammocks called corselets. Strapped securely into corselets, the birds couldn't injure themselves on a rocking boat. Pam placed Odessa gently into a corselet and fastened the basket over her own shoulders.

She planned on sending Odessa with a message so that Mama wouldn't worry about her when she discovered Pam's deception, as she surely would. Mama would be riled as a winter storm with Pam for fibbing, but at least she wouldn't be sick with worry on top of it. Of course, there would be some punishment awaiting Pam when she got home, but Pam wasn't going to worry about that now.

Judging by the way Pam's stomach growled, it was along about noon before she and Odessa were paddling toward the swamp. Pam pushed through the slow, brown water against a current that sucked hungrily at green-lichened rocks.

She wasn't sure *exactly* where Sanders' place was. She remembered that it was up one of the small creeks that branched from the cypress swamp Papa called the Little Dismal, as opposed to the Great Dismal, which spanned the North Carolina–Virginia line north of Currituck. Although Pam and Papa had camped in Sanders' dilapidated cabin on overnight hunting trips, Pam had never paid close attention to how they got there. She usually had her mind on their hunting, or on the sights and sounds of the swamp: turtles sunning on cypress knees, fish snapping at the fly hatch, herons and kingfishers and osprey, even an

occasional gator lazing on the muddy bank. The swamp
was a world unto itself, a world that Pam respected and
loved. But today there was no time for idle observation.
She had to concentrate on finding her way to Sanders'
cabin—and quickly—because another storm was gathering.
She could feel it in the air and see it in the way the leaves
turned their undersides to the wind.

By the time the canoe skimmed into the Little Dismal,
the swamp did indeed look dismal, even creepy. Slate-
colored clouds had gobbled up the sun, and the water was
inky black. In the twisted cypress knees Pam could see the
shapes of gnomes and dwarfs and every kind of creature
she had read about in Grimms' fairy tales. The cicadas
buzzed, and somewhere in the belly of the forest a wildcat
screamed. As Pam paddled deeper into the swamp, a mist
began to rise and snake through the trees. Some animal
rustled a holly bush onshore. Pam couldn't shake off the
feeling of being watched, though she knew the swamp
wasn't haunted; that was superstitious mumbo jumbo. Still,
when the *oo-whoo-oo* of a dove drifted across the dark
water, Pam shivered and paddled harder.

At the mouth of each small creek, she scanned the bank
for a familiar landmark. She remembered a huge tree on
Sanders' creek that Papa had always remarked on, though
she couldn't for the life of her recollect what kind of tree
it was. *I'll know it when I see it,* she kept telling herself.

And she did. It was the largest cypress tree she had

ever seen—its trunk was at least seven feet around, and its bulbous knees protruded another fifty. Confident now, Pam paddled up the narrow creek, poling in places that were too shallow for paddling.

She found Sanders' cabin on the edge of the creek. It was built of pine logs, now grown over with moss and lichens and hugged by maidenhair ferns. It had once sat in a clearing, but the sweet gums and pines had encroached on it. Virginia creeper wound up its walls, and poison ivy tangled with trumpet vines on its roof. Its windows gaped like lifeless eyes.

"Don't look like nobody's setting up housekeeping here," Pam said aloud. Her voice rang through the stillness. She banked the canoe and walked around to the front of the cabin. The door stood slightly ajar. When she tried to push it open, it stuck at first, and when she pushed harder, the door caved in and she crashed onto the cabin floor. Odessa in her basket on Pam's back squawked in alarm, and something hairy bumped against Pam's face.

Pam screamed and flailed her arms against her attacker. *Chirr-chirr*, she heard behind her. She turned in time to see a mother raccoon with a kit in her mouth scurrying through the gaping doorway.

Pam crawled to her feet and gazed around. The inside of the cabin looked as desolate as the outside. Clearly no one had been living here, at least no one human. From their nest in the fireplace, the remaining raccoon kits squeaked for their mother. Pam knew their mama would return. But their pitiful cries echoed the desperation building in Pam's own chest.

Here she had expected to find her pigeons, to nail Arminger once and for all. Instead, all she found was an empty cabin and a nest of brokenhearted babies.

She unstrapped Odessa's basket and eased herself to the floor to think. Arminger wasn't living here; Arminger wasn't building here; Pam didn't think Arminger had even *been* here. A chill started creeping over her as she realized that Arminger had intentionally deceived everyone in Currituck.

But why?

Because he really is a spy.

The answer suggested itself with perfect logic in Pam's mind. Her heart hammered as the significance of those words pierced her understanding.

That would mean that Mama was wrong about Arminger's being a decent person . . . wrong about there being nothing to spy on in Currituck.

And if Mama could be wrong about that, maybe she could be wrong about other things. Like the reason they weren't getting letters from Papa.

Pam felt like a spider dangling above a chasm on one thin string. For she knew, if all this was true about Arminger, his presence in Currituck spelled danger—to American soldiers, to Papa, to everything she held dear.

Back outside the cabin, Pam scribbled a note to let Mama know she was safe. She rolled the note up and slipped it into the cylinder-shaped tube fastened on Odessa's leg. Then she tossed Odessa into the air and watched her float upward into the charcoal sky. The bird circled once, flapped her wings vigorously, and disappeared. At the exact same moment, a wolf howled deep in the swamp. The tree frogs and cicadas rumbled, and a great cavern of loneliness opened inside of Pam. She had the feeling she was the last human being on the face of the earth.

Later, paddling hard through the black swamp, Pam barely felt the rain on her neck, barely felt the cold night-mist rising. Her emotions boiled inside. She felt betrayed and angry and scared, all at once. Arminger had pretended to be a friend to her, and to the whole town, all the while plotting against them. It was more than Pam could handle alone. She would have to tell Mama everything she knew.

It was late when Pam hit Scuppernong Creek. The rain had stopped, the stars had emerged, and a wedge of moon had slinked into the trees. Pam let the current carry her downstream. By then her brain had gone numb. The black trees glided past like figures in a dream. At her own landing Pam somehow found the strength to hoist the canoe onto the bank and stumble up the rise to the house.

A single light burned in the back of the house—Mama's room. Pam's heart twisted at the thought of Mama, rocking for hours, pretending to read her Bible but worried to distraction over Pam. Apprehension gnawed at her. How would Mama react to her disobedient daughter's home-coming?

Pam crept into the dark kitchen. On the stove Mama had saved supper for her: Irish potatoes, field peas, and cabbage. Pam remembered that she hadn't eaten since the sweet potato in early afternoon, but her stomach turned at the thought of food. A floorboard creaked under her foot.

"Pam? Is that you?" A halo of light appeared at the end of the hall, then Mama's ashen face in the doorway. Her long brown hair was disheveled and there were dark circles under her eyes.

"Yes, ma'am," Pam croaked. Her throat was too tight to say more.

Mama set the lamp on the kitchen table. She looked old. "Child, where have you been?" Her voice was shaking.

"Didn't you get Odessa's message?" Pam asked. She felt suddenly limp, and she grasped the edge of the table to steady herself. She wanted to fall into Mama's arms, but she wasn't sure how she would be received. Was Mama mad or fixing to cry?

"Yes, but that was hours ago. I been worried half to death." Mama's voice broke then, and Pam collapsed against her. Mama held her close. Pam breathed in Mama's smell—soap sweetened with bayberry, wood smoke, sun-dried linen. Mama's deep voice crooned, "Child, child, what on earth's got into you? Running off like that, telling tales, playing hooky, shirking your chores." Mama sounded like her heart was breaking at the extent of Pam's sins. Then her tone changed, scolding, severe. "Your papa would whip you good for half of what you done today."

The reprimand cut into Pam like a knife. She'd been trying not to cry; now sobs poured from deep inside. She told Mama everything.

Mama listened in silence, but her lips were set tight. When Pam finished, Mama said quietly, "I don't want you repeating none of this to anybody, you hear?"

For an awful moment Pam thought Mama didn't believe her. "It's true, Mama, all of it. I swear. We got to do something."

"I'm not doubting you, sugarfoot. But this is serious business, making accusations of spying. It's clear the man lied. Why, we don't know. We can't up and report him as a spy for telling falsehoods. Let me think on it a spell, over the weekend. Come Monday, I'll figure what to do.

"For now, you got to eat you some supper. Then you can answer for disobeying me and locking your dog up in the barn."

Pam gasped. She'd been so all-fired set on getting out to Sanders' place, she'd forgotten to let Bosporus out of the barn. "Mama, I—"

"I ain't interested in your excuses, Pam. The very idea of letting a wild dog in our barn, with a newborn calf in the stall. He could've killed that little calf with no trouble at all. And Mattie, well, he scared her half to death, poor thing. She already had a terrible head cold from being caught out in that storm." Mama shook her head. "I pray she don't give it to Iva or those twins."

"Mama," Pam said, annoyed with her mother's straying from the subject, "Mattie's scared of Bosporus anyway, for no reason."

"Well, she had reason this afternoon." Mama's voice betrayed irritation. "He startled her when she opened the barn door. I heard her hollering, and by the time I run out there, he had her backed up against the barn door, growling. I had to pull him away."

"So where is Bosporus now?" Pam asked, her mouth dry. She was almost afraid to hear the answer.

"Oh, he lit out into the woods, good thing for him. Luckily he hadn't touched the calf."

Pam was indignant. "Bosporus would *never* hurt Pyrenees. You know how good he is around my pigeons."

Mama's tone softened a little. "You do work wonders with your critters, honey, but the dog is wild, and wild animals are unpredictable. You don't really know what he would do. We can't sit idle till he seriously hurts someone. Or kills 'em. He's going to have to go, one way or another—tomorrow." Her voice was as firm as hard-packed clay.

There was no doubt in Pam's mind that Mama's patience with Bosporus had run out. And she knew what Mama's "one way or another" meant. If Bosporus wasn't gone tomorrow, Mama would shoot him. Pam felt cold all over as she forced her tongue to move. "I'll take him off tomorrow, Mama, way back in the swamp where Papa and I used to go deer hunting. There's all kinds of caves and hollow trees, and plenty of rabbits to chase, and a great big old pond with ducks. He'll be so happy, he'll forget all about us." She swallowed a lump in her throat. "He won't come back. I promise."

That night Pam slept fitfully. She dreamed she was running through a forest of old, craggy oak trees, being chased by something—what, she didn't know. She kept thinking she'd be safe if she could get out of the woods to Currituck Sound, only she kept getting lost, and whatever was chasing her was getting closer. Her legs felt like dead weight; she could hardly lift them. Then she heard a shotgun blast, and she turned around, and the Hun from the poster was right behind her, grinning. He was carrying something under his arm, and he held it up for her to see. It was a pigeon, a dead pigeon. It was Caspian.

Pam woke up shaking.

After the nightmare, she couldn't go back to sleep for a long time. She lay in bed, staring at the map of Europe on her wall, wondering where Papa was now, if he was even alive. She must have drifted off finally, for the next

thing she knew the rooster was crowing and a pearl-gray
light sifted through the window.

Pam was out of the house before Mama was up. It was
a beautiful Saturday morning, the sky a pale blue and
every bird in creation singing. The air had a nip in it, as
fall mornings in Currituck do. A breeze from the creek
carried the tart smell of ripe grapes. How could the world
wake up so bright and cheery when Pam felt so dead
inside? Her last day with Bos and he didn't even suspect.
He was waiting for her as usual by the pigeon loft, his tail
whipping happily back and forth.

Somehow Pam wasn't surprised when she discovered
another pigeon missing, this time a young, untrained hen
named Toulouse. She figured Arminger would keep up his
pilfering until every one of her birds was gone. And she
was powerless to stop him, completely powerless.

If I'd sold them, she thought bitterly, *at least we'd have the
money.* The way it turned out, he got her birds and she got
nothing.

After breakfast, Pam set out in the canoe with
Bosporus in the bow and Odessa in her basket strapped
to Pam's back. Best to be prepared, Papa always said. She
pulled upstream for miles, until the creek wound into
gentle curves through a vast forest of long-leaf pines and
towering hardwoods.

"This is it," Pam said, rowing to the grassy bank.
Bosporus was out of the boat before Pam could get it

moored. Barking, he bounded into a copse of sparkleberry bushes and flushed out a covey of quail, then leaped half-way up a chestnut tree after a squirrel. Pam trudged after him, watching his antics with amusement but also with a heavy heart. She wondered if he would hate her for abandoning him, or if he would simply feel bewildered and betrayed. He'll get used to it, she told herself firmly.

The place Pam had in mind to leave Bosporus was a thickly wooded hummock on the edge of the Little Dismal, several hours' hike from here. Pam had brought food in a knapsack, some apples and buttermilk biscuits for her and Bos and some grain for Odessa. That, with a couple of bass from the pond, some sparkleberries and papaws, and she and Bos would feast like Christmas dinner. Pam would be home in time for supper, and she would leave some fish for Bos.

The woods chattered with squirrels—gray squirrels and silvery-black fox squirrels—and the blue jays and cardinals were jewels against the dark green of the pines. Bosporus ran here and there and yonder, Pam steering him slowly in the general direction she wanted to go. Once, a doe frisked out of the brush, eyeballed Pam, then bounded across the clearing and, with a flash of white tail, disappeared into a pine thicket.

The morning danced by more quickly than Pam wanted, and soon the piney hummock loomed in front of her like a bad dream. On the pond, cinnamon-brown and studded with lily pads, a pair of pintail ducks glided and dived.

Pam found a deep pool among the weeds where the bass bit like there was no tomorrow. She caught five two-pounders quickly, then built a fire and roasted them on a flat rock. After eating, she and Bosporus lazed in the shade and dozed. Pam woke up with Bos' head on her belly, and she ached inside with the pain of leaving him behind.

They took a walk around the pond. Pam wanted to show Bosporus the caves on the side of the hummock. She figured he could make a nice den out of one for the winter. He plunged into several, sniffing feverishly, and emerged with his tongue hanging out, looking pleased.

Pam dreaded the moment of betrayal she knew was fast approaching. When Bos cocked his ears and whipped off after a rabbit into a wild-grape thicket, Pam sprinted in the other direction. She half splashed, half swam through the pond to throw Bosporus off her scent. When she hit the opposite bank, she took off running. The pigeon basket bounced on her back, and Odessa quarreled at being jostled.

Pam ran wildly, in no certain direction, angry tears streaming down her face, hating everyone in general and Arminger and Mama in particular. She crashed through briars and leaped over rotting logs, paying no heed to the blood trickling down her scratched legs. When she tripped over a protruding root, she fell hard and bashed her knee on a stone. Odessa set up a racket, but there was

no way she could be injured strapped snugly in her corselet. Pam sprawled on the ground, gasping for breath, her
knee smarting and her head pounding, wishing she was
someone else—Nina, Louisa White, even Alice—someone
who had no dogs to betray and whose father was safe at
home. A hawk screamed overhead, and a woodpecker
hammered from high in a hickory tree. Pam felt weary to
her bones.

After a long time she rose and tried to figure out
where she was. She reckoned she had traveled southwest
from the pond about four miles. She was definitely in a
stretch of forest she didn't recognize. If she pushed hard
due east, in a couple of hours she should reach the creek.
Then she could follow the creek up to where the canoe
was moored.

So she started east—what she reckoned to be east—
through a thick beech grove peppered with pines and
holly and carpeted with running cedar. The day had
turned hot for October. There was not a whisper of a
breeze. She tried not to think, only to walk, to keep moving steadily east. It wasn't long before hunger was gnawing
at her belly, so she climbed a chinquapin tree and shook
down a bunch of its small, brown nuts.

That was when she noticed the gash of a newly cut
road twisting through the forest.

Which was peculiar enough in itself. Loggers had
never shown much interest in cutting the swamp timber-

land around Currituck, not when there were virgin stands of more easily accessible hardwoods stretching for acres and acres to the west.

And why on earth would anyone else trouble themselves to carve a road through this wilderness?

Pam slid down the tree to investigate.

What she found only heightened her curiosity. The road was deeply rutted with tire tracks. Fresh tire tracks.

Burning with interest, Pam followed the road as it wound northeast, deeper into the forest. Soon the trees—laurel and live oak, cedar and gangly pine—hugged so close no sunlight could penetrate their canopies. Only the ribbon of bare earth Pam followed was splashed by the late afternoon sun.

At last the road opened into a clearing, where wooden buildings were set in neat rows like Mama's kitchen garden. The buildings hadn't been there long. The odor of fresh-cut pine hung in the air . . . along with another smell, much more familiar to Pam.

Pigeons.

CHAPTER 10
A SPY'S HIDEOUT

 **P**am stood rooted to the ground, her pulse pounding. Maybe this was where Arminger *really* lived. Then her pigeons would be here too!

Suddenly the ground beneath Pam's feet began to tremble. Behind her, the trees shielding the road from view spit out the sound of a motor lumbering up the road. Someone was coming!

Pam dove out of sight into the foliage. She crouched in the brush, eyeing the road. Soon a truck rumbled into sight, and another, and another. Three trucks in all, with wooden crates stacked in their beds.

Pam watched them approach, holding her breath. The roar of their engines swallowed the woodland sounds. The lead truck thundered nearer, until it was close enough for Pam to confirm what she suspected. Her heart skipped a beat.

The driver of the truck was Arminger.

Pam's chest tightened. She couldn't breathe. She dropped to her haunches while her mind raced. It seemed she had what she wanted: Arminger, red-handed with her pigeons, and a passel of other people's pigeons to boot. But she felt so frightened she could hardly move.

The other engines growled past. Gathering her courage, Pam lifted her head barely above the leaves. The trucks had stopped in front of one of the buildings, and the men were unloading the crates and carrying them inside. They seemed to be taking great care with the handling. Pam's breathing quickened. What did they have in those crates?

Everything she'd heard and read about spies tumbled back upon her. Spies were everywhere, listening to every offhand comment, monitoring every newspaper report, gathering information on every street corner to use against America's war effort. They planted bombs under factories and government buildings, and tried to assassinate American leaders. Pam remembered word for word one particular CPI poster: Germans are like hunters studying their game, and for the same purpose. Their object is to kill. To kill. To kill.

Icy talons of fear clawed at Pam's spine. In those crates could be anything—weapons, poison gas, even bombs. The men had finished unloading and were standing outside, smoking and talking. Pam strained to hear their conversation, but she couldn't make out words.

Their voices were a low drone like the buzz of a horsefly. If only she dared to get closer. . . .

Minutes passed, or maybe it was hours, while Pam wrestled with herself—her cold fear versus her burning hatred for the likes of Arminger and his sons, if they were his sons at all. She was one girl against three men, all probably armed. If she got caught, there would be no one to come to her rescue; no one would even know she had been here. Arminger would go right on with his sinister plans, and no one would ever be the wiser.

In the end, Pam's fear won out. She couldn't bring herself to move any closer. Better to go home and get help, she told herself. She hoped it wasn't too late for that already.

Pam shivered. The midday heat had melted into the long shadows leaning across the road. It would be a race now to get back to the creek before dark. With her heart as heavy as an anvil, Pam turned into the woods and trotted east. She felt the sun weaker, yet still warm, on her back. Inside she was cold. She hated herself for giving in to fear. Not only had she abandoned her dog, she had also abandoned her pigeons. The stolen pigeons were right there under her nose—they had to be—and she was too much of a chicken to go after them.

Then and there Pam changed her mind. It was one thing to spy on spies, to eavesdrop on their conversation, to try to foil their plans—that was deadly stuff, not something one lone girl should get mixed up in. It would be another thing entirely to sneak in before dawn while the men were asleep and rescue her pigeons. She could be in and out of their compound in a flash, her birds strapped safely in corselets in her basket. Pam's confidence surged as the plan took shape in her mind. Odessa would fly with a message for Mama; Pam would spend the night in the woods and steal into the compound before first light.

Pam hiked a few miles further into the forest. She would have to be far enough away so that Arminger and his men couldn't see the smoke from her campfire. And she would have to have a fire; nightfall would bring cold, not enough to freeze a body but enough to make a body *feel* frozen.

Once she found a good spot to camp, Pam sent Odessa off to Mama. Then, using her belt hatchet and pocket-knife, Pam set up a reflector for her campfire—green pine logs split in half and stacked between posts with the flat side to the fire. The idea was to deflect the heat in her direction. For kindling she picked up cedar shavings, pine straw, and small twigs. Then she gathered fallen logs and branches and separated them into stacks according to size, the biggest logs for keeping the flames going through the night. She shingled together fresh-cut pine branches, overlapping the needles like shingles on a house, to make herself a mattress and a blanket. Maybe she wouldn't exactly be cozy in her spicy bed, but she'd be warm enough to sleep. All her senses would need to be alert tomorrow for her foray into Arminger's territory.

Having seen to her warmth for the night, Pam turned her attention to satisfying her empty belly. Between the wild chestnuts, chinquapins, papaws, and wrinkled yellow persimmons, the trees yielded enough food to ward off hunger pangs. Most of the berry bushes had been well-scavenged by coons and possums, but beside a little stream she found some muscadine grapes, which she had for dessert.

Soon dusk had dropped a blanket across the woods. The stars, one by one, pricked through and blinked cold and distant above Pam's head. To Pam the forest was a friendly place in the daytime, but nighttime transformed the trees into shadowy hulks where, she imagined, yellow-eyed creatures lurked in the darkness. The slightest noise, even the hoot of an owl, sent prickles down Pam's spine. If only Bos were here to protect her. . . .

Pam dozed on and off through the night. Once, the fire went out and she was awakened by her own shivering. It took a while to get the fire started again and for her to get warm enough to drift back off. Somewhere in the mid-night hours, a grunting sound broke into her sleep. She jerked awake and thought she was hearing Lula down in the barn. Then she remembered where she was, in the middle of a forest miles from home. She lay paralyzed by fear, listening to *something* grunting in the trees outside the clearing. She heard stamping and pounding, coming closer and closer; then terror seized her as something crashed headlong through the trees at the edge of her campsite and lumbered away into the night.

After that, she couldn't go back to sleep and didn't dare move to feed the dying fire. From the quiet, she judged dawn to be near, so she waited impatiently for the inky sky to fade to gray. She wanted enough light to find her way to Arminger's compound, but enough darkness to keep Arminger asleep in bed until she was safely away with her pigeons.

At last Pam rose stiffly from the ground. Her stomach was growling, but she was far too nervous to consider eating, even though she had saved some nuts from last night. When she stumbled over part of a deer's antler at the edge of the clearing, she scolded herself for her night terrors. Autumn was rutting season for the deer; last night's monster had been nothing more than two bucks fighting over a doe and the loser fleeing through the forest.

The hour or so before dawn is the only time a forest is truly still; the insects have quieted, the night-prowling creatures have returned to their dens, and the birds have not yet stirred. Every twig that snapped under Pam's feet seemed to echo through the silence like a drum.

When Pam reached the edge of the compound, faint traces of pink were showing in the east. Here and there a bird had begun to twitter. With the first kiss of real sunlight the trees would be alive with chatter, and Pam's opportunity would be past. She figured she had maybe thirty minutes to find her pigeons and get out.

The whitewashed buildings gleamed against the backdrop of the trees. As a ghostly half-light washed over the clearing, the outline of the buildings grew familiar. They were pigeon lofts, rows and rows of them. Anxiety pressed hard against Pam's chest. How would she ever find her pigeons among all these birds?

Careful to keep her movements slow and soundless, Pam crept into the nearest loft. The sleepy pigeons stirred on their roosts, making throaty sounds that soothed Pam's nervousness. In the presence of animals Pam never doubted herself. Her pigeons weren't in this particular loft, but she *would* find them; she was sure of it.

The next building was a breeding loft, lined on three walls with nesting compartments. Although Pam didn't expect to find her birds here—Arminger wouldn't have had time to mate them—she peered quickly into each nest box just to be sure. One overzealous father, eager to protect his youngsters, rushed at Pam and pecked her on the cheek.

Her hand flew to the wound. "Ooww!" she cried out. Pigeons boiled out of their boxes, fussing loudly at the disturbance. Immediately Pam froze, knowing they would calm as soon as they realized she was no threat to their babies. She prayed that Arminger and his comrades were heavy sleepers.

Once the birds were quiet, Pam tiptoed out and went on to the next loft and the next. Every building was the same: scores of slim, sleek homers, but not hers. As bright daylight seeped steadily into the clearing, Pam began to get worried. Arminger would surely be waking any time now, and she still had one more row of lofts to go through, those closest to Arminger's cabin.

She chided herself for saving these lofts for last. She should've searched them first, while she still had darkness as an ally. If anything happened in these lofts, like another irate pigeon attack, Arminger would hear the ruckus and come on the double. Pam's stomach churned as she debated whether to take the risk of checking these lofts. What kind of treatment could a trespasser expect at the hands of German spies?

Then she thought of Caspian with his sharp, fiery eyes, and Orleans, and little Toulouse, and she burned with determination to get them back. She had come this far. How much time could it take to search a few more lofts? Anyway, she had a feeling about one of the lofts, the second one in the row. It was the only one in the compound that was sheltered by myrtle bushes. Almost as if Arminger had set out to design a loft where her pigeons would feel at home. She had a hunch that was where she'd find her birds.

Confidently Pam stepped inside, but disappointment rushed over her as she realized the loft was filled with youngsters, hardly more than squeakers. Some were not even fully feathered. Why had she been such a fool as to think Arminger would take any pains to comfortably house the pigeons he had stolen? No telling what he had done with her birds. Maybe they weren't in the compound at all.

The thought plunged Pam into despair. What gave her the idea she could outwit a German spy? This whole expedition had been a waste of time. Mama would be furious with her, and Pam had put herself at risk for nothing. All for nothing. There was no use to even check the other lofts, nor was there time. Specks of dust were dancing merrily in the sunlight that streamed through the window.

Then Pam gasped. Footsteps, outside the loft! A voice, singing jauntily. It was Arminger!

Pam scanned the room, looking for a place to hide. In a pigeon loft? No such thing! She could hear the words to Arminger's song clearly, something in a foreign language. He was on the other side of the wall. Surely he could hear her heart pounding.

Panic washed over her in waves. If she didn't move now, *do something* . . . she didn't even want to think about it. Her only chance of escape was to run for the woods. In the woods she could hide; there were hundreds of places to hide.

If she could make it out of the compound.

Quickly she calculated her chances. She was an excellent runner, but she was only a girl. Arminger was a grown

man. And a spy. Wouldn't he as soon shoot you in the back
as look at you?

The footsteps came closer. They were right outside
the door. One more minute's hesitation and she'd be
caught. Pam hurled herself against the door with the force
of a hurricane. She startled someone, a man. He staggered
backward, cried out.

Pam streaked past, flew down the rows of white lofts.
She heard shouting behind her. Was it Arminger? Did he
have a gun? Her legs pumped.

Can't look back, she thought. Run. Run!

Doors slammed. Pigeons squawked. Feet pounded
behind her, gaining on her. Closer. Closer.

Arms seized her, pulled her to the ground.

Chapter 11
Captured!

The map on the wall was of Currituck. Pam had recognized it the second Arminger brought her into the cabin. Nothing on the map was labeled; there was only a series of oddly shaped rings and numbers scattered across its face. Pam was sure, though, it was meant to be Currituck. The bodies of water, the shoreline, the islands offshore called the outer banks — she recognized them all. She felt a chill in the marrow of her bones. What awful fate did Arminger plan for her home?

And what fate did he plan for her?

He hadn't treated her roughly, hadn't confined her in any way — yet. Only sat her down at the table and proceeded to putter at the stove, stoking the fire and setting the coffeepot on to boil. He sent his partners away, told them to wait outside. Pam wondered for what.

He got bread from the pie safe, sliced it, slid it in the oven to toast. He was whistling a tune Pam knew but couldn't quite place. He went back to the pie safe for jam, put it on the table. Tension mounted inside her like an incoming tide. Why was he ignoring her? Was it part of his tactic to wear her down, to break her by means of her own anxiety?

He took mugs from the cabinet—two—and poured steaming coffee into each. He pushed one across the table to Pam. She shoved it away.

"What? You don't drink coffee?"

Pam held her chin high. "I drink coffee. But not spies' coffee."

"Oh, I'm a spy, am I? And you the one prowling in *my* pigeon loft."

Pam's eyes flashed. "And you've been lying to everyone. About why you came here, where you're living, what you're using the lumber for—everything. You told me you were thinking of raising a few birds. You have hundreds. And your map." She cocked her head toward the wall. "It's Currituck. What is that for?"

Arminger made no attempt to answer. Instead he nodded slowly and sipped his coffee. Him so unflappable— it infuriated Pam. There was no use even trying to talk to him.

Then, suddenly, he leaped to his feet. Pam braced herself for a blow, but Arminger bounded in the other direction, toward the stove.

"The toast!" he exclaimed. He yanked the oven door

open to a cloud of black smoke. He grabbed the pan with his bare hands, then cursed in a foreign language when he burned himself. The bread, black as the smoke, slid off the pan and bounced to the floor. Arminger retrieved it and tossed it in the trash. The scene was comical, but Pam didn't laugh.

Arminger, sheepish, turned back to Pam. "Not much of a cook, am I? And that's all I had for you to eat. We planned to go to town first thing Monday for supplies."

"I'm not hungry," Pam replied stiffly.

"Not hungry. I see. That's the way it's going to be." Arminger sank to a chair and sucked his burned fingers. "Okay, the spy business then." He took a deep breath. "It's true I planted some misleading information around town about my business here—"

Pam cut him off. "Not misleading information. Lies."

"Yes. Lies. But necessary ones." He paused. "Yet lies and a map on a wall don't make spies." His eyes locked onto Pam's.

Pam thought of her own map and of the lies she had told in the last few days, and she squirmed a little. Like him, she had thought her lies necessary at the time. But the comparison stopped dead there. She was an American; he was a German. Let him try to explain that away. "Germans make spies," she said emphatically. "Your accent is German."

"So it is," Arminger said, without batting an eye. He

looked into his coffee for a second, then back up at Pam. "I can see how you would draw such a conclusion based on that evidence."

His confession threw Pam off guard. She had a sense of floundering in water above her head. "Then you are a spy," she heard herself say.

"Well," said Arminger, bracing himself on the table and half rising, "no."

He pushed his chair back and stood upright. He looked directly at Pam, but his eyes weren't focused and she had the feeling he was thinking very hard about something else and not seeing her. When his attention snapped back to her, his eyes were burning with intensity.

"It seems to me, Pam, that you're an extraordinary girl, and that's why I've decided to share some extraordinary information with you about our operation here. What we're doing here *is* classified, and it *is* very important for the war effort. And I *am* working for the government, but not a foreign one. My partners and I are working for the U.S. Army to develop a secret weapon—night-flying homing pigeons."

A rush of air heaved into Pam's lungs. Pigeons—a secret weapon! That would explain . . . but no! It was too far-fetched. This was just one more of his clever tricks—using her pride in her birds to take her in. She knew too much now to be so easily duped. "You just admitted you were German. Now I'm supposed to believe you're working for the American government. How simpleminded do you think I am?"

"You misunderstood me," he snapped. There was a fierce undertone in his voice. "I never said I was German. I'm as American as you are."

Then he sighed. "I'm sorry. It hasn't been easy through this war having my loyalty constantly questioned. I come from a group of people called the Pennsylvania Dutch. The *Dutch* is really *Deutsch,* which means German. They came here from Germany centuries ago, probably before your own ancestors, but their religion calls for them to seclude themselves from the world. They live in isolated communities, and many speak only German. Those of us who have left the faith can't shake our accents, as much as we would like to.

"I don't think you're simpleminded, Pam. Far from it. But I understand your not wanting to trust me. Let me show you something."

He strode over to a trunk that sat at the foot of one of the bunks and rummaged inside, then returned with a bulging folder, which he placed on the table in front of Pam. *Confidential* was stamped across the front.

Pam's pulse quickened. It looked official. And it was in English.

"Open it. Just to the first page," Arminger said. "The rest is classified."

Pam willed her fingers not to tremble as she lifted the

cover of the folder. Inside was a thick pamphlet marked in large letters *Property of U.S. Army: For Official Use Only.* Pam's heart began to race as her eyes skipped down to the small print below:

*Instructions
on Reception, Care and Training of Homing Pigeons
in Newly Installed Lofts of the Signal Corps, U.S. Army*

"What is this?" she asked, almost in a whisper.

"Orders directing our operation here. Our *secret* operation. Hence my need for an alibi, or my lies, as you call them. Currituck is a perfect location—isolated, yet near our source of supplies at the shipyards in Norfolk."

His eyes were animated. "Our little homing pigeons are remarkable creatures, yah? They'll fly hundreds of miles at incredible speeds across unfamiliar territory to return to their home. That makes them excellent messengers, as you know."

"But what would the army want with them?" Pam asked.

"Reliable message carriers are crucial to an army. Battle plans must be relayed from one unit to another, orders changed, distress signals sent—all kinds of things. A tiny pigeon flying high in the sky can get through where other messengers fail. The army considers homers vital to their communications, but pigeons have one weakness— a major one to armies fighting around the clock—and it's my mission to overcome it. You know what that weakness is, Pam."

A door flew open in Pam's mind as she understood. "You want night flyers."

"Yah. Yah," Arminger said, getting excited. "That's why I was so excited about discovering your birds. How much easier would my job be if I could breed from birds that already have this ability?"

This seemed a question not meant to be answered. Pam waited to hear more.

"The army considered me an expert pigeoneer, which is why I was drafted for this project. I, in turn, hand-picked my partners for their pigeon know-how. The three of us must take all these birds—over a hundred, and more coming every day from Norfolk—and turn the cream of the crop into night flyers, birds that can fly in the dark across all kinds of terrain. Hence the topographical map there"—he pointed—"showing the land formations and swamps around Currituck. Our night flyers will then be shipped to Europe to aid our boys in the trenches. Pigeons winging through the thick of battle with important messages have saved many lives in this war, Pam, and the night flyers we're raising here will save many, many more. Think of it. One of these birds could even save your own father's life."

Pam's mind was swimming. *These birds . . . save your father's life.* She wanted to say something, but words jumbled

themselves in her brain, and she was still too stunned
by Arminger's revelation to separate them. All she could
do was shake her head.

"Oh, I know it's a lot to hit you with all at once, but I
wanted you to understand why I felt I had to have your
birds."

His words angered Pam anew. Suddenly she found her
tongue. "Yes, sir, I understand how you felt, Mr. Arminger,
but that still didn't give you the right to steal the birds
after I wouldn't sell 'em to you."

Arminger looked baffled. "Steal them? I don't know
what you're talking about. I gave up on getting your
pigeons when you refused to sell them to me. Someone
else in town did offer to sell me some birds—said they
were better than yours—but the one bird I saw didn't
interest me; it was pretty ordinary. And I have access to
ordinary birds by the hundreds, as you can see." His eye-
brows knit together. "Your birds disappeared?"

"A few of 'em. My best ones. You remember Caspian,
the one that took a shine to you?"

"Yah. The red cock with the snappy eyes." He clucked
his tongue. "That's a shame. He had the makings of a
champion flyer. And you thought I had taken him. Which
is why you were prowling in my loft."

Pam felt herself blush. She pulled her eyes from his
and stared at a crack in the table. "Well . . . yes."

"You have no other suspects?"

Without looking up, Pam shook her head. Her face was burning with embarrassment. What a silly little child she'd been, jumping to one wild conclusion after another. Arminger was probably glad he hadn't done business with her. All she wanted now was to crawl out of here and get home to Mama. "Look, Mr. Arminger," she started, but he broke in.

"That's a shame, yah. About your bird. Perhaps you'll find him." It was the sort of offhand comment adults made when they were really thinking about something else.

Pam knew it didn't matter how she responded. "Yes, sir," she said, and waited.

"Pam." He paused, as if he was mulling his very decision to speak. When he spoke again, there was conviction in his voice. It reminded Pam of a preacher at a tent revival. "I'm a man of my word. I made a promise to your mother not to offer again to buy your birds, and I won't break that promise, even though I think you might consider selling now that you know our purpose. But the *eggs* of your night flyers . . . would you sell me those? On the condition, of course, that you come help train the squeakers?"

"Me?" Pam was flabbergasted. "You want me to train pigeons for the army?"

"Yah, to help. The techniques we've been experimenting with, you've already perfected. You could train us to train the birds. If you're willing."

Pam felt as if she'd stepped from a stifling room into an ocean breeze. Arminger thought enough of her ability with animals to ask for her help with his project! She was breathing so fast she could hardly reply. "Yes, sir, I'm willing," she managed to say. Then, as a happy pride washed over her, she exclaimed, "Wait until Henry Bagley hears about this! He'll never sneer at my birds again."

Alarm leaped onto Arminger's features. "No! This operation depends upon secrecy. No one but your mother can know. Understand?"

"Oh." For a moment she felt let down, but it didn't last. So what if she couldn't tell anyone? She would know inside herself that Mama had been right all along—her gift with animals was of value. The U.S. government thought so! "I can keep a secret," she said. "I won't tell a soul."

"Good. Then we're in business, if your mother agrees. I'll run you home in the truck right now and explain everything to her." Then, as if the thought had just occurred to him, he added, "How did you get out here anyway?"

"I took the canoe. It's moored on a creek a ways back in the woods. I'll need to take it on home, I reckon. Maybe you could come by later to talk to Mama."

"Yah," he said, nodding. "I have a Red Cross board meeting this afternoon in town. I'll stop by your place afterward."

❧

Pam's shoulders rose and fell mechanically as her paddle dipped into the creek's brown water and lifted again,
dipped and lifted. The current did most of the work—a
good thing, because her mind was miles away. Arminger's
words tossed about in her head:

*Someone else tried to sell me pigeons . . . said they were better
than yours.*

Who would make such a claim? she wondered. Every
year for as long as she could remember, the Lowder
pigeons had taken first prize at the county fair. Other
pigeon keepers in the county bought breeding stock from
her. They all knew Pam raised the best homers around.
Besides, the pigeon keepers were country folks; they all
lived even farther out in the boondocks than the Lowders.
They only came to town on Saturdays to shop, and that
rarely. They would have no way of knowing that Arminger
had been trying to buy her pigeons. Unless one of them
had just happened to be in town on a weekday, which was
unlikely.

Wait a minute! The thought hit Pam like a white
squall. Mama said Buell had been in town on the very day
that Arminger showed up asking about her pigeons! He
had even accepted a ride from Arminger to hunt for Doc
Weston. He could have known about Arminger's offer.
And he surely needed the money.

"But Buell would never claim his pigeons are better than mine," she said aloud. "He knows better. His birds are scarcely alive!"

Pam especially hated to think that one of the Suggses would steal from her; they'd been the Lowders' nearest neighbors as long as she could remember. Yet the more she pondered it, the harder it became to deny that the evidence pointed to Buell. And to cover himself if he was caught, he could always make up an alibi. *Like borrowing Papa's crab pots.*

Buell's guilt would even explain the cigarette butt outside the barn.

It all fit together, snug and tidy, like the pieces of a puzzle. Then why did Pam feel so dejected? There was nothing to do but go and confront Buell as soon as she got home and talked to Mama.

The sun was hot on Pam's back by the time she sighted her own landing. She made the canoe fast onshore and trudged up toward the house, all the time rehearsing in her head what she would say to Buell. There was just no easy way to accuse your neighbor of stealing.

Halfway up the rise she was jerked from her concentration by a shriek, then barking and hollering that came from somewhere near the pigeon loft. Through her mind raced a hundred thoughts at once, but two jumped out in front:

Bosporus was back.

And he had caught Buell stealing another bird.

Pam tore up the hill, her heart pounding faster with every thud of her feet on the sandy ground. What a relief it would be to finally catch Buell red-handed!

But her heart nearly stopped when she topped the rise. There was Bosporus, teeth bared, with *Henry* backed up against the storage shed.

CHAPTER 12
A BIRD IN HAND

For a minute Pam was frozen. A jay scolded from a bough above her head, and a squirrel chattered. A mix of emotions swirled inside her. Astonishment at seeing Henry instead of Buell. Joy that Bosporus had returned. Fear at what Mama might do to Bosporus.

Henry hollered louder, setting Bosporus into a frenzy of barking. Pam knew she had to move fast.

She sprinted the distance to the shed. "Bosporus!" she yelled. "Get down!" Bosporus looked at Pam the same way he did when he was pleased at himself for treeing a squirrel. He barked sharply.

"He's going to kill me!" Henry wailed. Bosporus growled.

"Hush, Henry. You're making him mad. Don't move."

She edged up on Bosporus. She didn't think he would hurt Henry—not really—but Mama's words rang in her head. *He's wild . . . unpredictable . . . you don't really know what he would do.* If Bos got a little too zealous guarding his "prey," or if Henry made a sudden move . . . Pam closed her mind against that thought.

Step by step she sidled closer, talking, crooning to Bosporus. "You're a fine dog, Bos, a fine dog. Look at what you done. Now hold still, boy. That's a boy. Hold—" and she grabbed the ruff of his neck, wrapped herself around him, and pulled him back. She winced more from guilt than pain as she felt the cockleburs in his fur pricking her. He glanced up at her with eyes so full of devotion and pride it wrenched her heart. Then he glanced back at Henry and growled menacingly.

That was when Mama came running up. Judging by her expression, she was plenty riled. "What's going on here?" she asked.

Henry looked daggers at Pam. "That dog tried to kill me!"

"He attacked you?" Mama was standing with her hands on her hips, which meant she was boiling mad.

Fear for Bosporus rumbled in Pam's stomach and began to inch up into her chest. She drew her dog closer. "Bos didn't even touch him, Mama."

Mama's eyes flashed fire at Pam. "I asked Henry." Her tone was razor sharp. "Did the dog bite you, Henry?"

Tension gripped Pam as she waited for him to answer. If Bos had bitten Henry, her dog was doomed; Mama

would insist he be put down. Nervously Pam scanned
Henry's bare arms, looking for the clean puncture of
canines. Sometimes such wounds didn't bleed.

Then she narrowed her eyes. Had Henry's coat pocket
wiggled? She blinked. There! It had wiggled again!

A thought crashed into her brain, like a tree plummet-
ing into a river. *Someone in town . . . pigeons to sell . . . better
than hers . . .*

"Henry Bagley, tell me what you've got in your pocket!"
Pam demanded.

Henry's mouth fell open, and a guilty look etched itself
across his face. From the loft a few yards away drifted soft
pigeon noises, but Pam heard something closer—a faint
groo-groo. And it sounded like it was coming from Henry's
pocket.

Mama heard it, and so did Henry. Pam saw it in their
faces. But before either of them could act, Pam moved
like a rattler striking. She shoved her hand into Henry's
pocket and pulled out a small, gray pigeon.

Odessa!

But Odessa looked pitiful. The iridescent feathers on
her neck were dull. Her feet had been bandaged; one wing
seemed to be broken, and there was a gash on her neck
where the feathers had been clipped away. She blinked up
at Pam and cooed weakly.

Fury welled up in Pam's throat, nearly choking her.
"What have you done to my pigeon?"

For once in his life, Henry appeared to be at a loss for words. His eyes darted to Mama, then to Bosporus, then to Pam. He stammered a few syllables.

Mama turned to Pam. "Well, I *don't* know what Odessa's doing in Henry's pocket, but I can explain what happened to your brave little pigeon, or what I think happened." She glowered at Henry. He looked away. "Henry and I found the poor thing this morning dragging herself into the pigeon yard. On foot. We figured she was attacked by a hawk and somehow got away, but couldn't fly home."

Pam had always suspected Odessa had more heart than any of her other birds. She stroked the bird's soft crown. "So you doctored her up?"

"Yes, and fed her real good and put her in her nest pan. Maybe Henry would like to explain the rest." Mama's tone said Henry had better make his story good.

"He don't have to explain. I *know* why he had Odessa. He was gonna steal her like he did my other birds and sell her to Mr. Arminger!"

"Pam!" Mama chided. "You got to quit pointin' fingers at people without proof."

"I know for a fact this time. I have proof, a witness."

"Where is this witness?" said Mama.

Pam stammered, "I . . . can't tell you right now."

"I don't know a thing about your stolen birds! I swear!" Henry protested.

"And I suppose you don't know a thing about how

Odessa got in your pocket," Pam shot back.

"It was a joke, to pay you back for getting me in trouble with Pa. I was only going to keep the bird in my pocket until you missed her and got a good scare, but then that mongrel attacked me—"

"He's lying, Mama. Alice warned me he said he'd get even with me. But I never thought he'd stoop to stealing."

"You threatened Pam?" Mama directed this to Henry.

"Not exactly," hedged Henry. "I might have said I'd teach her a lesson or something like that. I don't remember to a hair."

"You don't remember." Pam could tell Mama doubted Henry's memory loss. "I see."

Pam rushed in. "Mama, think about it. Henry's been here every time a bird showed up missing. And he knew from the start that Mr. Arminger wanted 'em bad. It adds up, don't you think?"

"I didn't take your dang pigeons!"

"Henry! That's enough," said Mama. She hesitated what seemed a long time to Pam, then heaved an enormous sigh. "I s'pose it does appear that Henry took your birds."

"Miz Lowder, I didn't!" Henry looked genuinely distressed. If the situation hadn't involved her pigeons, Pam might have enjoyed seeing Henry unsettled.

"I think the whole thing needs to be settled at your house, Henry, with your father and Alice there. We'll see if we can straighten things out," said Mama.

"Not today. Pa has a Red Cross board meeting at the house this afternoon."

"We'll be happy to wait till his meeting is over. It'll give me a chance to have a nice visit with your ma."

Pam marveled at the way Mama could find a courteous way of saying near about anything.

The Bagleys owned the biggest and one of the oldest houses in Currituck County. It was a two-story Federal built in 1762 by Mrs. Bagley's great-great-granddaddy, who made a fortune off shipping naval supplies like pine pitch and turpentine to England before the war. The house sat far back from the road in a willow grove.

Pam gasped when she saw Arminger's truck parked in front of the house. She hadn't realized that *his* meeting was Mr. Bagley's meeting.

Mrs. Bagley, still dressed in her Sunday frock, greeted them at the door and ushered them into the front hall. Its walls had wainscoting of cypress wood, and a cypress stairway led up to a landing above. Pam had been in the Bagleys' house a number of times, but Mrs. Bagley had never invited her past the hall. Pam always had the impression Mrs. Bagley looked down her nose at the Lowders.

Mama explained their errand.

"I don't think Henry's your thief, Mrs. Lowder. I'm

sure it was just one of his boyish pranks." Pam hated the
way Mrs. Bagley made a show of pronouncing *Mrs.* as
"missus" instead of "miz" like everyone else in Currituck
did. Probably she figured it set her above the common
folks like Pam and Mama.

"Still, I think it'd be best to air this out with everyone
at hand," insisted Mama.

"That's not possible," Mrs. Bagley countered. "As
director of the Red Cross, Ed must head up the meeting,
don't you know." Her tone dismissed them. She might as
well have opened the door and pushed them out onto the
veranda.

"We'll wait," said Mama firmly. She seated herself on
the Empire sofa set up against the wainscoting. Feeling
uncomfortable, Pam eased into a chair beside the sofa.
Mrs. Bagley stared coldly at them, but Mama didn't flinch.
Pride surged through Pam. Mrs. Bagley's snobbishness
was no match for Mama's determination.

Soon the parlor doors swung open, and the most
important citizens of Currituck emerged: Mr. Bagley,
Judge Patterson, Doc Weston, Sheriff Purdy, and Chester
McClees, who was head of the Farm Bureau. And, of
course, Mr. Arminger.

Mrs. Bagley glanced nervously at Pam and Mama, as if
they were a spot of mud on her carpet that she hoped no
one would notice. Before the men could do more than pay
the barest respects to Mama, Mrs. Bagley had herded them

into the dining room for "refreshments," which meant a full supper intended to show off the talents of Mandy, her cook. Once the guests were safely out of range, she whispered in Mr. Bagley's ear, stealing disapproving glances every now and again at Pam.

"I'll take care of it," Mr. Bagley assured her. With that settled, Mrs. Bagley rearranged her face, floated into the dining room, and closed the double doors.

Mr. Bagley cut a deadly look at Henry, who had planted himself sullenly on the stairs. "Fetch your sister," he ordered. Then to Mama he said, "Let's go in the parlor, Miz Lowder." As courtesy dictated, he held out his hand to help Mama up. Pam wondered why such a genuinely nice man had married someone like Mrs. Bagley. "I'm sure we can iron this thing out," he added.

Suddenly it occurred to Pam that no ironing out was necessary. The person who could prove her case was right here—Mr. Arminger! She pulled Mama aside and filled her in on the offer Mr. Arminger had received. "He's my witness, Mama. Henry won't dare fib in front of him."

Mama's face had remained impassive during Pam's tale, and Pam couldn't read her. Pam was eager to have Mr. Arminger back her up. "Can I go in and get him, Mama?"

"No, I'll speak to him myself. You go ahead and tell your story to Mr. Bagley. I won't be long."

It seemed to Pam that Mama was gone forever, though the grandfather clock in the parlor had only ticked out a quarter of an hour. It hadn't taken long for her to tell her side to Mr. Bagley, but then Alice and Henry began arguing over whether Henry had actually said he was going to get even or only hinted at it. Mr. Bagley seemed to think the story would be more fully told if his children were allowed to hash it out. Pam was getting impatient with the whole process. Where were Mama and Mr. Arminger?

Finally Mama returned with Arminger behind her. Pam's heart dropped when she saw Mama's face. Her mouth was set in a thin, straight line. "I'm sorry for not believing you, Henry," Mama said.

Pam's jaw dropped open. "But Mama—"

Mama shook her head. "It wasn't Henry who tried to sell birds to Mr. Arminger. It was a girl."

CHAPTER 13
HOMING IN

Arminger's truck rumbled to a stop in the Lowders' front yard. Arminger jumped out and came around to help Mama descend from the dizzying height of the bench seat. "I appreciate your letting Pam come help me, Mrs. Lowder. May I pick her up Saturday morning, early?"

"That'd be just fine, Mr. Arminger. I'm sure Pam's rarin' to get started."

"So am I," he said. "See you then, Pam?"

"Yes, sir. Early." She grimaced as the truck roared off, kicking up a cloud of sand.

Mama shuddered. "Lordy, them motor trucks make my bones rattle, don't they yours?"

"Yes'm," Pam said idly. She had her mind on Mr. Arminger's description of the girl who had brought him a pigeon in a basket on Wednesday afternoon. A skinny little thing, he had said, with white hair and the palest blue eyes he had ever seen. And she was barefoot. "Mama, you know as well as I do who Mr. Arminger was describing."

Mama sighed. "Mattie. It can't be no one else. But I don't understand it. It don't make sense."

"Yes, it does. I figured it out on the ride home." Pam told Mama about her original theory that Buell was the thief. "I only changed my mind because I thought we caught Henry red-handed. Now I'm convinced Buell stole my birds. He must've made Mattie talk to Mr. Arminger to throw suspicion off him."

"I hate to think that of Buell," Mama said. "He's always so protective of Mattie."

"I got to go over there and face him down, Mama. Else he's liable to keep right on helping himself to my pigeons."

"I don't know, Pam. Likely I should talk to Iva about it, though I'm loath to worry her any more in her condition."

"Then let me go and handle it my way. Please?"

"All right. But be careful you don't get riled and spout off. Be as obliging as you can under the circumstances. Remember the strain Buell's under with his pa gone. Hear?"

"Yes, ma'am." There was still one more thing Pam wanted to ask, and she didn't quite know how to phrase it. "Mama. My dog." She hesitated, struggling with the words. "Ain't he shown you he's a good watchdog and not vicious? Can't he stay?"

Mama looked at her intently. "It's true he didn't hurt Henry one whit. And there's no doubt he's loyal to you, traipsing all that way through the woods to come back to you. We'll give him one more chance. How's that?"

Pam took Bosporus and went the back way to the Suggs place, up the creek a ways, through a sedge field, and past a pond where a family of mallards swam. Once on Mr. Eugene's land—land tended by the Suggses—she noticed how run-down everything had gotten. Pope bushes grew thick in all the fields, and dog fennel had taken over the barbwire fences. She wondered if Mr. Eugene would put the Suggses out and try to find another tenant who would keep the place up. Pity for Buell's plight tugged at her, but she hardened herself against it. Being dirt-poor didn't give him the right to steal from her.

There was a reason she took such a roundabout route. She was hoping to avoid running into Buell until she could get a look at his pigeon shed to see if her birds were there. How could he deny taking Caspian and Orleans and Toulouse if they were sitting right in his shed?

Up through the bare tobacco fields Pam and Bosporus went, past the Suggses' smokehouse and the corncrib, to the edge of the old pecan grove where Buell had his rabbit hutches and his bird shed.

"Dang!" Pam said when she saw Buell cleaning out his pigeon shed. "No way to check up on him first. Reckon we'll have to plunge right in, boy." She held tight to the scruff of Bosporus' neck. It wouldn't do to have him lunge at Buell; Mama had only given him one more chance, after all.

"Buell Suggs," she sang out.

Buell glanced up. "Mattie ain't out here, Pam. Did you hunt for her in the house?"

"Ain't looking for Mattie. I come to see you."

Buell's face darkened. "Listen, I done told you to leave off pestering me about what I feed my birds. 'Tain't none of your business."

"I don't care if you feed your birds chicken droppings. I got a bone to pick with you."

"Oh yeah?"

Buell stood up straight and looked at Pam through narrowed eyes. Pam's heart drummed in her chest. Buell towered over her. Why hadn't she let Mama come with her? She swallowed hard. No, this was her fight, and she could handle it. Mustering all her courage, she opened her mouth to speak. Then she clamped it shut. She had just noticed something. Bosporus' tail was thumping against her leg. Bosporus was looking straight at Buell . . . and wagging his tail!

Buell squatted and snapped his fingers toward the dog. "Com'ere, boy. You know me." Bos trotted right to him, and Buell scratched his neck. "Bet he's got some wolf in 'im with them blue eyes of his, you reckon?" He stroked the dog's flank. "Now what's this bone you got with me, girl?"

Pam was speechless. Bos went to Buell like a cricket to a hearth. If Buell was the pigeon thief, why wasn't Bosporus all flustered like he'd been with Arminger and Henry? It didn't add up. Maybe Buell wasn't the thief after all. Her mind raced. What could she say to him now? "Why ain't you returned Papa's crab pots?" she croaked. It was all she could think of.

Buell looked at her funny. "Your mama told me I could keep 'em as long as I needed 'em."

I'm making a fool of myself. Again, Pam thought.

Then a rumble escaped Bos's throat, and his lips quivered so his teeth showed. Pam heard the thud of footsteps behind her, and leaves crunching. She turned. It was Mattie.

"I saw you from the window," Mattie said. "I had to wait till Ma left the kitchen 'fore I could sneak out." She was breathing hard and coughing.

"You all right, Mat?" Buell asked, concern in his voice.

"Yep," she said, coughing harder. "That cold's done settled in my chest, is all. I'll be fine directly."

Bosporus growled again, louder, and stepped forward. Buell ruffled his fur. "Simmer down, boy. What's wrong with him?" he asked Pam.

"I don't know." Pam was watching the dog, watching how his eyes were fastened on Mattie. "He is acting queer, don't you think, Mattie?"

It was as if Mattie had just noticed him. "What's that dog doin' here? Thought you got rid of him." She eyed him warily. "Don't let him near me. He don't like me."

"Why don't he like you, Mattie?" said Pam. "He likes Buell fine."

Suddenly Bosporus barked and leaped forward. Mattie jumped back and squealed. Pam dropped quickly to one knee and fastened her arms around the dog's neck. She stroked him as she talked. "Mama changed her mind about getting rid of Bos. He turned out to be too good a watchdog. He sure did. You should've seen what he done to Henry Bagley when he caught him taking one of my pigeons."

"What?" Mattie's voice was trembling.

"And that stranger in town, that Mr. Arminger, why all he had to do was *look* like he was going to swipe a pigeon," Pam went on. "Bos lit out after him so fast, it was all I could do to hold him back. And you know, it's funny; dogs never forget. I reckon he'll go after Henry every time he sees him now." She paused. "But you got nothing to fear from him, Mattie." Pam's eyes locked onto Mattie's. "Do you?"

Mattie licked her lips. She coughed. Another rumble escaped Bosporus' throat. Suddenly he strained against Pam's arms. Mattie cried out and cowered. "I didn't *aim* to take your birds, Pam," she whined. "If Buell's bird hadn't up and died on me—"

At last Pam knew the truth. She felt a surge of relief—
at first. Then anger at Mattie began to build in the pit of
her stomach. She saw the pleading in Mattie's eyes, but
Pam didn't feel like being forgiving. Not after what she
had been through in the last few days. Not before she got
a dang good explanation for Mattie's actions. "You stole
my birds, Mattie? Why?"

Mattie winced at the word *stole*. It was the common
excuse of many landlords whose overworked land wasn't
producing: *My tenants are stealing me blind.* Pam felt a pang
of guilt at using the word, knowing Mattie would be sensitive to it, but she felt it only for an instant. She wasn't a
landlord and Mattie wasn't her tenant, and Mattie *had*
stolen from her. It was as simple as that. Pam waited in
stony silence for Mattie to speak.

"I didn't aim to," Mattie insisted. "It's just . . . well . . .
the day Ma took sick, Buell come home full of tales about
that foreigner with the motor truck offering you a fortune
for your pigeons. I told Buell we oughtta sell *his* pigeons
to the man."

"And I told you he wouldn't want my pigeons," Buell
cut in.

"Yeah, but you wouldn't tell me why not," Mattie shot
back. "You told me to mind my own business."

"Well, why *didn't* you?" said Buell.

"'Cause. The way I seen it, a pigeon is a pigeon. I
thought you was being stubborn, so I decided I'd take a

pigeon to the man myself. I figured you'd be so happy,
Buell, 'bout all the money I got us, you wouldn't even be
riled at me for takin' it." Here Mattie's eyes sparkled. Pam
knew her well enough to know Mattie had been already
spending that money in her mind.

"I sneaked off while Ma and the twins was sleeping
and walked all the way into town with a pigeon and found
that feller. But Buell was right. The man wouldn't buy it.
Then on the way home"—she glanced at Buell with apprehension in her eyes—"it died somehow, in its basket. I
knew Buell'd be mad as a hornet when he learnt I'd kilt his
pigeon, and I didn't know what to do.

"That was 'long about the time I was passing by your
place, Pam, and the idea come to me, all of a sudden, that
you wasn't likely to miss one li'l pigeon amongst that passel you got. If I took one of yours that looked like Buell's,
maybe he wouldn't notice the difference. I seen a nice
black one like I wanted a-sittin' outside in that wired-off
part of your pigeon pen, but when I started to pry the
wire off to grab him, that dog come a-runnin' up barking.
I hightailed it for the storage shed and locked myself in
till he went away. Then I climbed out the back window
and hid up in your hayloft. After dark I went back in the
pouring-down rain and grabbed a black pigeon. Don't
know if it was the same one or not; you got so *many*. I
figured you wouldn't even notice it was gone, Pam."

Mattie's eyes looked enormous in her thin, pale face.

Pam knew she was seeking forgiveness, but Pam wasn't ready to give it. What made Mattie think she could up and take her birds just because Pam had a lot of them?

Then Buell voiced her own thoughts. "Mattie, just 'cause a body's got a passel of something don't oblige you to help yourself to their belongings. That's same as stealing."

"Oh, I aimed to bring him back directly, soon as I figured a way to tell you what happened," Mattie said. "But then me and the bird spent the night together out in our barn—it was so late I was afraid Ma would catch me sneaking in and light into me—and that thing cuddled up to me and cooed like he was so content, and he felt so silky and warm, well, in the morning I . . . I couldn't bear to turn him over to you. I couldn't. So I fixed him up an old rabbit hutch and hid it in the tobacco barn. I was only gonna keep him a little while."

"That's why you was so eager to take care of my pigeons for me," said Buell. "So I wouldn't notice one gone."

"Yeah, I figured I'd keep that up till I could bring myself to part with Blackie. That's what I named him—Blackie. Then he started acting poorly, like he was pining for his pigeon friends. And I knew how he felt, and I didn't want him to be lonely, so I went back and took more pigeons to keep him company. I know it weren't right, but I never aimed to give you grief, Pam." She lowered her eyes, and her voice got very small. "I reckon I was looking to have something of my very own for once."

Pam felt herself being pulled two ways. On the one hand, she sympathized with Mattie. No one knew better than Pam how comforting an animal could be, especially to a lonely girl whose father had been snatched away by war. On the other hand, she couldn't quite release her anger. She still wanted to chew Mattie out, but she didn't have the heart. Not with Mattie standing there fiddling with the hem of her dress and looking like an orphaned puppy.

"'Course, I know that don't excuse what I done," said Mattie. "You're my friend, Pam, and it ain't right to hanker for all the things you got."

Mattie's words caught Pam off guard. "I don't know what you could hanker for that *I* got. We ain't that much better off than you."

"For one thing, you got all them critters you can call your own."

"But you don't even like animals," said Pam.

Mattie shrugged her shoulders. "I might. If they was mine." She paused. "You got your ma all to yourself and time of your own to do what you want. And you go to school, and have your own friends there." Then she added sadly, "And you get your own letters from your pa, and you can read 'em."

Mattie thought Pam was privileged? It was a new thought to Pam, and she turned it over in her mind. Maybe she wasn't so poor after all, despite what Henry Bagley said.

The wind picked up then and rustled the few brittle leaves still clinging to the pecan branches. Mattie's hair stirred with the breeze, and Pam felt her anger starting to slip away. Mattie had put her through a lot of grief, but look what had happened as a result. Pam never would have discovered Arminger's compound if she hadn't been searching for her missing pigeons. In a way, she owed Mattie. It all depended on how you looked at it.

Mattie thought she was privileged? Then why shouldn't she share what she had with Mattie? Pam stroked Bosporus absently as she weighed the words she wanted to say.

Buell must have taken her silence as ill will. He stepped over beside Mattie and put a hand on his sister's shoulder. "We stand ready to make amends to you, Pam. She'll give you your pigeons back, and you can have all mine to boot. And I'll come over and help out your ma in the evenings, till you figure I've worked off the damage. Suggs is honest folks. You know that."

Buell's gesture touched Pam. It made her all the more certain that what she had decided to do was the right thing. "No need for that. What Mattie did wasn't right, but I reckon I can see my way clear to forgiving her. Under one condition."

"I'll never go near your pigeons again, Pam. I swear."

"Oh, but you're gonna have to." Pam tried to make her voice sound severe. "In fact, you're gonna need to be over there every day, so plan on it."

"What? You want me to clean your bird shed for you? Water the birds, stuff like that?"

"It's called a loft, Mattie, not a shed. You're gonna have to get used to calling things by the right name. And no, I don't want you to tend my birds. You won't have time. You'll be too busy tending yours. Squeakers take a lot of work."

"What's a squeaker?" Mattie asked.

"A baby pigeon, you dunce. Pam's offering to give you some baby pigeons of your own—I think." Buell looked at Pam uncertainly.

Pam nodded. "But you're gonna have to take care of 'em right, Mattie. Feed 'em right." She shot a look at Buell. "Handle 'em right, so they'll mind you and trust you."

Mattie's eyes were shining. "I'm gonna have baby pigeons of my own?"

"Not ordinary pigeons, Mattie. Night flyers. And if you come over every day and let me teach you how to train 'em, they might end up being . . . well . . . maybe the *second-best* night flyers in the county!"

1918

A Peek into
the Past

LOOKING BACK: 1918

Children playing on the main street of their hometown around 1918

In 1918, most Americans lived on farms or in small towns or villages. If you lived in a small town like Currituck, the outside world would have seemed very far away. News and letters traveled slowly. The radio, or "wireless," was so new that few families had one. Telephone service was not available in most rural areas. People didn't travel much. They grew up, married, raised families, and died within a few miles of where they were born. In your town everyone would have known everyone else. The arrival of a stranger like Mr. Arminger really would have been big news.

But when America entered World War I on April 6, 1917, the outside world began to touch all Americans' lives, as fathers, husbands, and brothers—like Pam's papa—left home to fight in Europe. There the war had already been raging for three years. It began with the murder of a prince in Austria-Hungary. Europe at that time was divided into two military partnerships: the Allies (Great Britain,

France, and Russia) and the Central Powers (Germany, Austria-Hungary, and Italy). If one of the countries was attacked, its partners would fight, too. Within weeks of the prince's murder, all the major countries in Europe were at war. Eventually more than 25 nations around the world joined in.

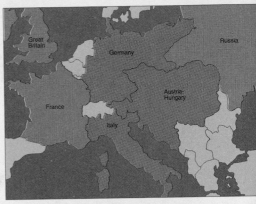

This map of Europe shows the Allies in yellow and the Central Powers in red.

At first the United States vowed to stay out of the war. But Americans became outraged at Germany's attacks on civilians, especially the sinking of the British passenger ship *Lusitania*. Finally, Congress declared war. Every American man of fighting age had to register for military service. If he didn't, he could be sent to jail. Wealthy businessmen signed up as soldiers, and so did illiterate tenant farmers like Ralph Suggs. Once in the army, men who had never traveled 50 miles from home were sailing thousands of miles across the Atlantic Ocean to fight.

American soldiers wave good-bye as a train takes them off to war.

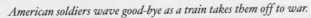

144

World War I soldiers going "over the top" into battle

Our dough-boys (the nickname for American foot soldiers) joined Allied forces already dug into *trenches*, complex systems of ditches made to protect soldiers from enemy gunfire. Soldiers spent months living in these ditches, waiting for the call to go "over the top"—to pour out of the trenches and fight. The area between battling trenches was known as *no-man's-land*. Soldiers who entered this scarred wasteland faced enemy cannon, machine-gun fire, barbed wire, and poison gas attacks that left men blind, paralyzed, or dead.

Troops in the trenches needed some way to communicate with their commanders, who were often stationed 50 miles or more from the battlefront. The outcome of a battle might depend on a single message reaching command posts quickly. Often soldiers relied on homing pigeons to carry these vital messages.

The birds wore aluminum tubes on their legs to hold coded messages, sketches, or maps. Both the Allies and the Central Powers used pigeons with great success—the birds delivered 95 percent of their messages safely. Pigeons were tossed from trenches, tanks, planes, balloons, and ships. Even spies used them.

A soldier holds a homing pigeon as a message is being attached to its leg.

Cher Ami

Many birds were wounded by enemy gunfire. The loss of an eye or leg was common, but injuries rarely stopped these brave little messengers from completing a mission. An example is Cher Ami, a black checker cock with the American army at the Battle of Argonne in France. German troops had completely surrounded Cher Ami's battalion. Cher Ami, the Americans' last pigeon, was their only hope for rescue. His leg was shot off by the enemy, but he still flew on to deliver his message—with his message holder hanging by a tendon. Thanks to his brave flight, the American soldiers were saved.

Pigeons had only one drawback as wartime messengers—they would not fly at night. So the U.S. Army began secret experiments to develop night-flying pigeons. Agents like Mr. Arminger chose 1,200 privately owned pigeons to be trained in government lofts. Four hundred birds eventually learned to home at night, and

This photo shows soldiers building lofts for night-flying pigeons near a battlefield in France.

they were bred to produce night flyers for the war.

While American soldiers, along with their pigeons, fought in Europe, at home the United States government waged another kind of war—a propaganda war. *Propaganda*

Government posters showed terrifying images of German, or "Hun," soldiers.

is information intended to make people support a cause or point of view. During World War I, a government agency called the Committee on Public Information, or the CPI, used propaganda to rally Americans to support the war. The CPI whipped patriotism to a fever pitch by planting frightening images of German soldiers in Americans' minds. The agency distributed millions of pamphlets and posters—many, like the one Pam saw, showing German soldiers as cruel or evil. Other posters warned that German agents lurked everywhere, trying to gain information to use against American troops. Citizens were told to report possible spies to the CPI, just as Miz Gracie wanted to report Mr. Arminger.

Prejudice against Germans and other foreigners erupted throughout the United States, especially in areas where many immigrants lived. Leaders of German-American communities were threatened or run out of town. People of German heritage lost their jobs and property. Some were even killed. Anything German was banned, even the performance of music by German composers who had died centuries before! Most German-Americans were loyal citizens, but the prejudice against them lasted long after the war ended with Germany's defeat on November 11, 1918.

A march against German-Americans in 1917

*During the war, women took over men's jobs—
from the railroads to the New York stock exchange.*

No battles were fought on American
soil, yet the Great War changed the face of our nation.
Cities grew as people left farms and villages. Many women
who held wartime jobs found new independence. Along
with thousands of returning soldiers, they moved to cities
to attend college or take jobs in offices and factories. For
the first time in America, girls like Pam could dream of a
future beyond their small town.

After the war, many Americans moved to cities to find more opportunities and excitement.

ABOUT THE AUTHOR

Elizabeth McDavid Jones has lived most of her life in North Carolina, usually near woods and creeks. Her earliest passions were animals—especially dogs and horses—and writing. She combined her passions by writing stories about animals. When she was ten, she and her best friend wrote a mystery about twin sisters whose twin horses were stolen. The story was almost one hundred pages long. Today, she lives with her husband and four children in Greenville, North Carolina, near a creek.

Free catalogue!

Welcome to a world that's all yours—because it's filled with the things girls love! Beautiful dolls that capture your heart. Books that send your imagination soaring. And games and pastimes that make being a girl great!

For your free American Girl® catalogue, return this postcard, call 1-800-845-0005, or visit our Web site at americangirl.com.

American Girl

Send me a catalogue:

Girl's name _____ / / ____ Birth date

Address _____

City _____ State ___ Zip

E-mail _____

( ) _____
Phone ❏ Home ❏ Work

Parent's signature _____ 120749i

Send my friend a catalogue:

Name _____

Address _____

City _____ State ___ Zip

113249i

Try it risk-free!

American Girl® magazine is especially for girls 8 and up. Send for your preview issue today! Mail this card to receive a risk-free preview issue and start your one-year subscription. For just $19.95, you'll receive 6 bimonthly issues in all! If you don't love it right away, just write "cancel" on the invoice and return it to us. The preview issue is yours to keep, free!

Send bill to: (please print)

Adult's name _____

Address _____

City _____ State ___ Zip

Adult's signature _____

Send magazine to: (please print)

Girl's name _____ / / ____ Birth date

Address _____

City _____ State ___ Zip

Guarantee: You may cancel at any time for a full refund. Allow 4–6 weeks for first issue. Non-U.S. subscriptions $24 U.S., prepaid only.
© Copyright 2001 Pleasant Company

K21L1